A YOUNG ADULT MYSTERY

SECRETS IN TIME

IVY LIGHTON

This is a work of fiction. Names, characters, organizations, places, events, and incidents are either products of the author's imagination or are used fictitiously.

ISBN: 9798398230031

Cover design and book formatting by Susan Healy VonAchen

Printed in the United States of America

DEDICATION

To my late husband, George, who sadly didn't stick around long enough to see me finish this. Thank you for reading the entire first draft and for your invaluable suggestions and support. Your spirit has encouraged me to 'write on' in your absence.

You'll be glad to know ...*the book is finally done!*

ONE

SPRING 1924

DAISY

A far cry from being a certified seamstress after one sewing class, Daisy was eager to create something on her own. She missed the stylish clothing which was all the rage in the 1970s, especially the jumpsuits worn by the iconic model Twiggy. Styles she was eager to wear when she entered junior high.

I can create a jumpsuit, like the one Charla (my mother in my previous life) wore. I'm sure of it.

Excitedly, Daisy flew down the stairs to the living room where Katherine's Singer stood prominently in the sunlight shining through the open living room window of their 1920s cottage.

A spring breeze blew the curtains in and out, allowing the fresh smell of the river and blooming spring flowers to pass through. It was a quiet Saturday afternoon and her parents would be gone for several hours.

Daisy opened the drawer of the sewing cabinet and removed a pair of scissors, then hurried back upstairs to her loft, climbing the steps two at a time.

She pulled a horribly outdated ankle length plaid dress from her pine wardrobe and laid it out on her bed. "Frumpy! Who would ever wear this?

Exhaling, she secured her braids together at the top of her head and pushed up the sleeves of her shirt. She cut the skirt from the bottom, vertically up the middle, almost to the waist.

After several fittings to check accuracy, Daisy went back downstairs to the sewing machine and sewed two seams to form wide legged trousers which flared from the knee.

If memory serves me correctly, yes, I think I've replicated the trendy style from 1970! She squealed with excitement.

Daisy was delighted with her bell bottom jumpsuit. She had a feeling her parents would oppose the pants, but she hoped they would support her progressive fashion sense.

She tapped her foot on the floor while she rehearsed her presentation in her head. Thinking about their reactions gave her butterflies in her stomach.

Maybe I'd be better off not showing them at all, and just wear it when they're not home. Hmm.

After mulling it over for thirty minutes, this teenage tailor sucked-it-up and modeled her new jumpsuit.

"What in heaven's name are you wearing Daisy Wilhelm?" Katherine questioned. "Did you destroy your plaid dress?" "It's a bell bottom jumpsuit." Daisy wondered how much trouble she'd be getting into. "Wherever would you get such an idea?"

Daisy swayed back and forth, biting on her lip. Her heart raced a little as she stood waiting for more criticism. "I assumed when I was teaching you how to sew you would make a dress for your 8th grade dance. Not something outrageous like this!" Katherine shook her head. "Please do not wear this 'jumpsuit' as you call it, to school or any formal gatherings. Do you understand?" "Yes, ma'am."

"So ridiculous! This child has such an imagination," proclaimed Katherine to Mr. Wilhelm. He had nothing more to offer than a mere shrug of his shoulders.

May 16, 1924

Dear Diary,

I've been here two years and doubt I'll ever adapt to the odd fashion style of this era! Growing up in the 70s was different from today. I'm STILL having a hard time trying to fit in. Girls here don't wear pants!! CRAZY, right? Luckily Katherine gave me sewing lessons, so I made myself a jumpsuit like the ones my mother Charla wore. It's not perfect, but I like it. And it reminds me of where I came from.

Daisy

Two

SPRING 1972

MEL

A ray of morning sunlight leaked through the rips in the tattered old curtains which hung on the only window in Mel's bedroom. A smile filled her face as soon as she opened her eyes. Excited about the sixth grade field trip and Mel's first ever visit to an animal sanctuary.

In her twelve years, Mel hadn't been to many places. The most fun she experienced took place at the playground around the corner. Mel looked forward to the day she'd go somewhere special with Charla. But the song always sounded the same when she asked. "We'll go soon," her mother would say. Then, Mel would cross her arms and reply in a huff, "One day I'll have a best friend. We'll go all the places and do all the things." And off she'd go to pout and sulk in the comfort of her bedroom.

Mel lacked brothers or sisters, or a close friend. And she never became close to the neighborhood kids. To have a very best friend would mean the world to her.

Mel pushed the orange and pink floral blankets aside and rolled out of bed. The terrazzo floor was cold on her feet so she slipped on the socks laying there from yesterday. Then, as she did every morning, she'd get herself ready while mommy dearest stayed in bed with a hangover.

Mel walked over to the closet and moaned at the limited choices. Hanging on the first hook was a lime colored polyester shift-dress with a pattern of scattered daisies. To her delight, the flowers concealed any sign of wrinkles from the last time the dress was worn. *A little short for me, but I don't have any better options.*

She slipped it over her head and tied a lilac colored sash around her tiny waist to add a fashionable touch. In the dress pocket, she found a single piece of Bazooka gum and a Spearmint Chapstick. "These can stay." She stuffed them back in and sauntered into the bathroom.

Mel brushed her caramel hair and styled it into two pigtails. She tied them up with the fancy new ponytail holders, which were being saved for a special occasion. Mel was used to doing her own styling, and pigtails were effortless.

She studied her face in the mirror, fascinated by the color of her eyes. The blue one inherited from her mother and the brown from her father. Charla's narrative, anyway. Mel had no recollection of the man's facial features.

How could anyone leave their baby daughter and never come back? An unanswered nagging question.

One last thing to do before heading out the door. Fix a bag lunch. She hurried down the stairs, passing the scarcely decorated living room. No family photos on the wall; just a giant poster of The Miracle Mets, 1969, which came with the house, and Charla left it up. "The poster will stay there until we have new art to hang," she promised. But that day never came.

Mel entered the kitchen and recalled what her teacher, Mrs. Bartlett, told the class. "Everyone will have to bring their own lunch for the picnic at the sanctuary."

Mel, who was short for her age, used a footstool to reach the upper cabinets. She opened one door and then another. Next, the fridge, looking for anything edible before searching the breadbox.

She took the last slice of rye and smeared it with a dab of grape jelly. *Better than nothing.* Mel thought if she ever found a Yoo-hoo chocolate drink or a Ding Dong cake to add to her lunchbox it would be a miracle.

❦

Most people who knew Mel would say she possessed a unique sparkle. An unexplainable vibe that positively brightened up the space. At a young age she learned to conceal her true feelings, and became an expert at hiding her shame from a dysfunctional home life.

Mrs. Bartlett knew the family history and sympathized with her. Whenever possible she'd give Mel an easy chore to complete and in return would sneak a candy bar or cookie into her lunch box. The other students had no idea.

Today, Mrs. Bartlett asked Mel to be the line helper on the field trip to Jungle Habitat. The safari was situated on 900 acres and housed over 100 animal exhibits and 1,500 animals. There was a lot of ground to cover, but Mel accepted her task. "Sure you don't mind being at the end of the line for the entire day?" Asked Mrs. Bartlett. "Oh, I don't mind at all." Mel enjoyed helping.

Her task was simple enough. Stay near the back of the line and observe the students up front. If anyone lingered, she would give them a little nudge to keep the line moving.

At twelve years old, Mel acted more like a teacher's assistant than a student. An effortless task, that made her feel needed.

⁓℮⁓

Several miles from the sanctuary hiding out in the forest, Marty gathered his gear into a big pile. Camping in the forest under the live oak trees was a family tradition important for cleansing the soul. He did this several times a year and in the past slept like a baby. But not last night. He tossed and turned round-the-clock, thinking about the betrayal of his ex.

"She thinks I don't know where the two of them live." He let out a heavy sigh. "Well Charla, you ticked me off for the last time, and today I'll settle the score."

Marty rolled up his sleeping bag and tossed the bedroll next to the wall with his other belongings. Unshaven and wearing the worn out clothing from the day before he headed in the direction of the zoo.

⁓℮⁓

Mel wanted to visit the baboons first, but the majority of the class chose the peacock pen to be their first exhibit.

"Hi." The strange man spoke in a husky voice, showing his nicotine-stained teeth when he grinned. *Ew.* Mel thought, but returned a bashful smile out of politeness before turning her head back to the peacocks.

Her smile seemed to be his opening to further engage in conversation. "Would you like a boost up to see them better?" He asked. Mel cocked her head to the side to indicate she wasn't sure. "Or you can wait a few years until you're taller." He snickered and leaned in closer. "I'm here now. Whadda ya say?" He was creepy, but she felt pressured, so agreed to the lift.

Thirty seconds later, Mel agonized over her decision. Without a word, a sweaty hand covered her mouth as he scooped her up and carried her away. She was terrified, but unable to scream.

While the peacocks entertained her classmates and other onlookers with their array of elaborate feathers, the abduction went unnoticed.

Marty carried Mel around the side of a building, out of view.

Ten minutes passed before her teacher or the other kids even noticed her missing. Several people nearby heard the commotion and scattered to search the area.

Mrs. Bartlett stayed behind with the children, who were all shuffling around and talking to one another. "Shush...! This is important! Did anyone see where Melissa went? Was she talking to anyone? Laura? Kim? You girls stood next to her." "Yes, maybe. I saw a man talking to her about the peacocks," mumbled Kim. "But I didn't see anything else."

THREE

THE ABDUCTION

The man sprinted through the trees, holding Mel against his hip. She slipped several times, but each time Marty shifted her up again and held tighter, bunching up her dress with each tug. Her bare legs swayed as she kicked. It wasn't until the two were deep in the woods that he let her down and forced her to walk while he pulled her along by her hand.

Dread twisted deep in her gut. Marty hadn't heard any police sirens yet and assumed they were far enough away for anyone to hear the girl's screams. "I do not intend to hurt you, kid. You'll see. So stop crying."

About three miles in, both exhausted, they reached a large stone wall which spanned a half acre. A six foot high, circular structure with an eight foot wide ledge. It was surrounded by trees and nearly hidden by the moss and overgrown vegetation.

Through tear-covered eyes, Mel surveyed the wall with interest. She remembered her school trip to Waterloo Village. They learned about the Native Americans who were the first inhabitants of the area. This place bared a strong resemblance to something she had seen in the exhibit.

Still pulling her by one hand, Marty dragged Mel

around the perimeter of the curved wall until they came to a large opening which resembled a doorway. The perfect hiding spot for a man on the run.

Leading the way, they walked to the area where she spied a disorderly stack of items against the inner wall. A sleeping bag, a jacket, a lantern, a knapsack, and remnants of a fire pit.

The thickness of the trees filtered out virtually all of the sunlight, and Mel was terrified.

Her tired legs shook, and struggled to hold her up. She collapsed onto the damp musty ground beneath while Marty picked through the knapsack with his free hand.

He pulled out a thick rope and an iron stake.

He yanked her arm, pulling her body up and pushing Mel against the wall. "Stand here," he ordered. The pain from the impact shot through her back. She tried to catch her breath before her neck slumped forward. "Look, I'm sorry. I wasn't trying to hurt you," he muttered.

The man roused her with a tap on her face. His fingers felt like rough sandpaper.

Eyes still closed, Mel lifted her head and leaned against the wall. He ran two fingers across her cheek. "Open your eyes."

He grabbed hold of her leg while he hammered a stake into the ground at the edge of the wall, loosening several of the old bricks. Next, he secured the rope around the stake and tied the rope tight to her ankle.

"Stop crying!" He insisted. "I'm not going to hurt you as long as you behave. Just do what I say."

His words escaped notice. Fear overwhelmed Mel, and the tears were uncontrollable. She wiped her eyes and nose with the back of her hand while trying to catch her breath. *Why me?* She dug her loose foot into the acorns which were scattered on the ground.

The forest grew darker and the air cooler. The thickness of the trees muffled any distant traffic noise. The inability to remain standing caused Mel's body to slide down the wall until she landed on the ground. Every last tear depleted.

Mel drifted off to a deep sleep while Marty walked around to the side of a tree to relieve himself of the two beers he drank. He glanced over to confirm the girl was still chained and sleeping. He hated having to resort to these measures. "She'll understand soon enough," he whispered. "And hopefully won't resent me." He glanced in her direction, then zipped his pants.

Thirty minutes later, Mel woke up. Disoriented, but

a little less exhausted than earlier. She looked over at the kidnapper, who was pacing back and forth near the trees, flailing his arms around. Her destiny was now in the hands of a monster. She never expected this.

Mel kicked the wall in a tantrum like style, which loosened a few bricks. "Ow!" The pain to her foot was extreme, but it didn't stop her from kicking the wall again until another brick fell out.

Marty looked over at her to double-check she was still secured to the stake. Then continued pacing a 10 foot area back and forth and mumbling to himself. This behavior lasted a while. Finally in his custody, but what to do next?

All he could think about was getting even with the back stabbing she-devil who called him a destructive influence. "Never good enough for her," he mumbled. "Or the kid."

Mel kept kicking away until another brick dropped and then another one. The activity was a good distraction from her grim situation and her hunger pains. Mrs. Bartlett collected everyone's lunch bags when they arrived at Jungle Habitat and the last time Mel ate was supper the night before.

Marty glanced in her direction, eyes squinted, wondering what the heck the girl was trying to accomplish. "You trying to break a foot?" Taking a brief rest from his pacing, he yelled in her direction.

She stopped for a few minutes to catch her breath.

"At least she wasn't screaming," he muttered.

And then she was back at it. In her moment of grief, she decided to fight her way out of adversity. With each kick, another brick fell and a good size hole was forming. It intrigued her.

The loosened bricks uncovered a hollow space big

enough to hide something in. *Maybe heirlooms or treasures of some sort were hidden in here at one time.* She visualized ancient artifacts, gold coins, gemstones, bones, and crouched down for a better view.

The way I feel right now — If this hole were bigger, I would crawl inside to die.

At that moment her eyes caught sight of something with a glistening sparkle far inside the space. She blinked for a reality check, then got on her knees for an even closer look.

Mel stuck her arm deep into the back of the hole, stretching as far as she could. *If my arms were a little longer, I'd be able to grab whatever it is.* She pushed another brick out of the way and another to widen the hole, in order to squeeze her head and shoulders into the musty space. She held her breath while she stretched her body to reach closer until she touched the treasure with the tip of her fingers.

"Hey! Kid! What the actual heck are you doing?"

Marty's husky, rumbling tone of voice frightened her enough to scurry deeper into the hole, but with one leg still fastened to the stake in the ground, she didn't get very far.

He reached in and grabbed her foot, but she kicked and he lost grip. "Daggonit! You're as cussed as your mother," he shouted.

Moving fast, she dug her fingers into the floor of the hole and wiggled her body a few inches deeper. *I got it!* A smooth stone about the size of an egg. Mel could feel a tingling sensation in her hand from the heat the sparkles were giving off.

Marty attempted to grab hold of her leg again. But this time his fingers lost their tight grip when an explosive force from inside the hole pushed him backwards three feet.

Mel was launched out right after and landed on the ground in front of him.

His rage erupted!

Then, suddenly, out of nowhere, a turbulent wind whirled around them. The sky darkened and lightning struck in the distance.

From the earth below, a cylinder of fluorescent yellow dust formed, expanding into a miniature tornado illuminated by the night.

It circled around the girl's hands and grew to envelop her entire body.

Marty watched in horror as the girl appeared to get sucked up by the funnel. The wind abruptly ceased, and his daughter vanished along with the storm.

A Special Gift is Revealed

Marty froze with horror. He'd never believe what happened if he hadn't seen with his own eyes. As many times as he heard stories of his ancestors creating time hop portals, he never imagined his daughter inherited the gift.

"How is it possible she'd have this ability and I don't?" He pulled at his unruly mane in frustration. "Could it be something else? Was she in the grip of some mysterious power?

Damned be those ancient rituals and the rocks they left behind! That gift is nothing but a curse."

Four

SPRING 1922

IS IT SAFE TO COME OUT?

Mel woke up on the hard terrain beneath an oak. She opened her eyes and looked around. Her mind lost in uncertainty. *Where am I?* She stood up and brushed the dirt off the back of her dress with her hand. Her white Keds covered in dirt and scuffed. Images of what happened the day before flashed in her mind, although nothing made sense.

She remembered being carried by the perpetrator into the forest. His sweaty hand covered her mouth, leaving the taste of salt and tobacco to linger on her lips. She spit. *Where is he?* Her chest rose in and out with each quick breath.

Mel needed to determine her whereabouts. *Where on earth am I and how did I get here?*

She walked a few yards in one direction and took another look around. Standing in the middle of a thick forest absent of a clear path leading to this location. *So strange.* Panic struck like a thunderbolt.

She blinked her eyes to clear the tears and recalled being carried to a giant wall made of old stones. *Where is the wall?*

Visually exploring the area, not minding her steps, Mel tripped over a large rock and brushed up against a fallen log. *Ow, that stings.* She bent down to rub her leg and noticed a bruise which encircled her ankle. Through the murk of her memories, a thought came to her. *Must be from the chain he tied around my leg. How did it come loose?*

Mel sat down on a little patch of grass just big enough for her to sit if she tucked her legs beneath. She closed her eyes and pressed on her brain. *Think Mel, think!*

She recalled the trip to the animal sanctuary going terribly wrong. And how she found a hidden stone in the wall, and crawled inside to grab it. *I wonder where that stone is now?*

She made her way back to where she was sitting when she first woke up and examined every nearby inch looking for the rock with no luck. *Am I imagining the events that brought me here?*

~~~

Charles Wilhelm finished his coffee and placed the empty cup on the kitchen counter. "Katherine, if you're not going to eat, won't you have a cup of coffee at least?" "Not right now. I appreciate your concern, Charles, but I'm not feeling well." "Oh, Katherine, it's been three years. I miss her too." Katherine's frustration was apparent.

"This anniversary is always hard for me, you know how I feel. I'll put it behind me tomorrow, I promise." Charles replied, "Maybe it's time we try again?"

Charles was a patient husband, and he adored his wife. He had a soothing voice, which normally helped when a little persuasion was called for. But not today. "I know you weren't ready to talk about this the last time I brought it up, but do you think we can try to have a conversation in the near future?" Katherine gave him a slight smile and a reassuring nod, and then Charles took her face in his hands and gave her a kiss on the cheek.

"I'll be at Live Oak Park most of the day." Her eyes held his gaze. "There's a lot of ground to cover and the developers need photos asap. I'll try my best to be home on time for supper," he said, before picking up his camera bag and walking out the front door.

Katherine stared out the kitchen window at the tire swing hanging from a tree. She wiped her tears with the apron which was still tied around her waist and walked outside.

Mel thought to herself as she wandered around Live Oak Park. *It would be in my best interest to stand out of plain view in case I'm being followed.* She looked around until she found a tree with large leaves and thick branches that curved toward the ground. A perfect place to hide while she thought out her plan. *I'll go this way through the forest and search for a trail out of here.* Mel drew the plan in the air with her finger.

She meandered through the various collections of trees in the forest. The stately Live Oaks, Elms, and Pine trees. Clearing the path of any stray branches before they struck her head.

The woods were incredibly silent. The only thing louder than her breathing was the noise the leaves and sticks made when they snapped under her feet. She worried someone would hear, so she slowed down her pace and tiptoed.

After a brief walk, Mel noticed something coming from a distance and paused to listen. *There it is again. It sounds like a dog barking. Maybe there's a house nearby. I wonder if someone is watching me?*

Fear set in and she questioned whether or not to go in a different direction. *I better keep on this path so I get out of here before nightfall.* She reasoned getting lost in a dark forest would be terrifying, so she continued walking and crossed her fingers she made the right decision.

Mel kept close to the trees to avoid being seen by anyone in the area. Every few minutes she'd look around to make sure she wasn't being followed. She listened for other sounds such as car traffic or people talking. Still, the only audible sound resembled an animal in distress.

She crouched down next to a blueberry bush, and grabbed a big handful of berries to eat. After filling her belly, Mel explored the forest further.

She passed under a wondrous live oak tree, which she guessed could be a hundred years old. And then, all of a sudden, the trees cleared to a wide open grassy meadow and Mel sighed in relief.

There it is! The dog was tied to one of the birch trees which stood about ten yards from the riverbank.

She approached carefully as to not startle the animal, then moved around it slowly. It whined louder and Mel's instincts told her something wasn't right. *Who would tie up a dog and then leave?* Mel looked into the distance as far as she could see. Squinting her eyes from the bright sun. The dog barked again. *Who left you here? We're gonna find them, okay? Don't worry.* She wanted to lean in and pet the animal, but she didn't.

Another bark prompted Mel not to give up. *It would be terrible to leave a dog all alone out here in the meadow. Maybe something bad happened to the dog's human.*

There was a river about 50 yards away which she hadn't yet checked, so she walked to the boundary where the grassy area ended and the slope to the river started.

Mel looked down to survey the area and saw a man lying at the bottom of the slope. She gasped at first and squinted her eyes to confirm her uncertainty, but relaxed when she realized he wasn't dead. His clothes were kinda weird she thought. A white shirt with gray pinstripe pants and suspenders. A large, funny-shaped camera was by his side.

The man looked up at her and called out. "My foot is trapped under this tree limb. Can you get help? The man, roughly 30 years old, spoke with a strained tone. "Take Finney with you. She knows the route."

Mel rushed to untie the dog and hurried to find help, returning thirty minutes later, with several men who happened to be nearby cutting trees. They were able to climb down the slope and pull the heavy tree limb off the man's leg.

By this time, Mel was even more suspicious by the day's series of unexpected twists, and asked herself again. *Why is all this weird stuff happening to me?*

After the rescue, the lumberjacks left the scene and Mel remained sitting in the grass, legs bent, elbows on knees, her head rested in her hands. Thinking.

The smell of dog breath made her lift her head just in time for a sloppy kiss from Finney. Mel smiled at the dog.

"Hello little lady, I'm Charles Wilhelm." He stood over her. "Finney and I are thrilled you came along today." Mel looked up at the man with a huge curiosity about his weird old-fashioned clothing.

Her arms hugged her body as she remained seated on the ground, reluctant to communicate with a stranger.

"And what may I call you?" He asked. But Mel just stared at him without a reply.

"Thank you for helping with the rescue. If you hadn't come along when you did, I may have drowned at high tide. You saved my life, young lady. And I don't know how long Finney would have lasted tied to a tree before someone found her. You saved us both!"

She looked up at him and squinted, which caused her forehead to wrinkle. Then took in a deep calming breath, and nodded, unaware of the magnitude of her help.

He inquired if she was lost, who she was with, where her mother was, how she got there. All the questions. But still, she remained silent.

He leaned in closer. "I'd like to help you if you'll let me. Finney and I can walk you home if you tell me where you live." Mel kept her lips shut until Finney, tail wagging, licked her cheek and she giggled.

Charles held out his hand to help her up. She smoothed over the daisies on her dress to get rid of the creases and stood up on her own. Two days worth of forest dirt covered her from head to toe. Both pigtails were hidden under an unkempt mound of hair.

Charles sensed she felt comfortable with Finney, so he asked, "will you take Finney's leash for me? She seems to like you and I bet she'll enjoy walking beside you again." Mel took the leash and walked alongside Charles.

"Now, let's get you home. Do you know your address?" She shrugged her shoulders. "If you don't tell me your name, I'll have to call you Daisy for now." Her eyes followed his finger as he pointed at the flowers on her dress. Her lips split into a smile.

Holding Finney's leash took her mind off things temporarily. Until vivid recollections of the animal sanctuary came back, and questions and concerns swirled in her head. She trembled, and the leash fell.

"Are you alright?" Asked Charles. He picked up the leash and handed it back to Mel and they continued at a slower pace.

As they walked through the forest in the same direction from which she came earlier that day, Mel spotted a giant stone wall. She furrowed her brows as someone would when they were curious. *How did I miss that earlier?*

As they got closer, she questioned if it was the same place the kidnapper took her, except it appeared to be different in certain ways.

The wall is missing the moss overgrowth. And yesterday there were acorns covering the ground with hardly a blade of grass peeking through.

The uncertainty persisted. *It could be the same place.* Her breath came in short gasps.

She leaned over and gave Finney a scratch on the neck, which was returned with an affectionate lick to Mel's face, raising a giggle. Still, Mel couldn't shake the visions of what happened to her yesterday. She remembered the sparkly stone that she searched for earlier.

I need to find that stone. If I do, I'll know where I am.

She pointed to the wall and looked up at Charles. "Do you live over that way?" He asked. She shook her head no but veered in that direction, anyway. She walked a little quicker, and Finney took that as a cue to run. The leash tugged and pulled her along with it. Charles quickened his step and followed.

"There it is!" She yelled in a whisper and ran over to snatch "her" rock off the ground, which she stuck into her pocket with the ChapStick and Bubble Gum.

"Oh, so you do talk! Now we're making progress!" The sound of her voice diverted his attention and he made no notice of her picking up the rock. "There what is?" He asked.

Mel realized she spoke before she was ready to be friendly with a stranger. For the next 15 minutes she remained quiet, until she heard him say, "you know you have a pretty sparkle in your eyes? I'm sure you've heard that before." She replied softly, "Yes, because they're two different colors." Charles smiled, but was troubled that he knew nothing else about this lost little girl.

"Sorry it's such a long walk into town. Think you can hold up just a few minutes longer?" He asked and she nodded yes.

"I'll bring you to my house and introduce you to Katherine, my wife. You may be more comfortable talking with a woman." He rambled on. "Your parents must be very worried. Are you sure you won't tell me where you live?" *"He asked a lot of questions,"* she thought.

They turned onto the main road and walked along the river. Mel's forehead wrinkled as she peered at the old style cars on the road and the buildings. All of it, unrecognizable except for the paper mill where her mom's boyfriend worked. She remembered driving past it once and Charla pointing it out. Mel studied the building as they passed. It looked much smaller, but the sign on the front is still the same.

"Where are we?" She asked. "Why, we're in Rutherford. The Passaic River is there, beyond the trees. And if you look down the road you'll see the river cottages where Katherine and I live."

"And, your children, too?" Interrupted Mel. Charles gazed downward, as if he was deep in thought. He looked in her direction and said, "uh, no, Daisy, we haven't any children." The sadness in his eyes was unmistakable. "Just Finney."

FIVE

WE'LL CALL YOU DAISY

"You can drop the leash now. She loves sprinting to the door and entering first. It's a game we play." The screen door to the cottage screeched open, and they entered the little hallway just outside the living room. Mel looked all around at the unfamiliar space. Her first impression of the cottage's interior were the drab colors and old fashioned style of decor.

Katherine, a tall woman with a friendly face, and much younger than Charles, walked into the living room, wiping her hands on her apron as she approached.

"Katherine's job was to manage the household." Charles explained. "This woman right here bakes the most delicious cakes and takes care of the cooking and cleaning, the laundry, grocery shopping, and sewing. I don't know what I'd do without my Kat." He leaned in and kissed his wife on her cheek.

"You're home early. And just in time for lunch." Katherine spoke in the most melodic voice.

"Oh my, who do we have here?" She took notice of Mel and leaned in to be eye level with her. "Aren't you the sweetest? Might I ask your name?" Mel did not reply. She gave Katherine the same dazed expression she had on her face most of the morning.

"We're calling her Daisy for now." Charles gave a wink. "She's a hero, Katherine. This brave young lady here saved my life today." Katherine's eyes opened wide with interest. "What? What do you mean, she saved your life?" Charles reassured her in a calming voice, "don't be alarmed. I'll tell you the entire story at lunch."

Katherine gave him a weird eye. "Okay then, you two, let's eat lunch and you can tell me all about it." They followed her to the kitchen table. "But first, how bout we get those hands washed, shall we?" She motioned for Mel to come with her over to the sink.

They ate vegetable soup and freshly baked bread with butter. Starving, Mel gobbled hers up, and Katherine served her another bowl while Charles spent the next half hour talking about his morning encounter and near death experience.

"She appeared out of nowhere. A miracle really." Mel chimed in, "I heard a dog barking, so I followed the sound until I got close enough to be certain."

Katherine reasoned that the girl's parents must be upset and perhaps searching for her.

She didn't want to burden the child with too many questions right now, so she refrained from asking anything more than what her name was. "Daisy, can you tell me your name? It's okay to tell us." Katherine assured her. "We'd like to help you find your family." Daisy looked up from her soup then shoveled a scoop of broth into her mouth.

"We need to get the sheriff and report this as soon as possible, for Daisy's sake." Explained Katherine. "Yes, I agree. As soon as we're done eating, you can get Daisy cleaned up and let her rest a little. I'm sure she's tired. And I'll go down to the pay phone to make the call."

Katherine voiced her opinion as she cleared the table.

"It's about time we hooked up a phone in this house. Half of our neighbors have one." She placed the plates in the sink and turned to face him. "I don't know why you think we don't need one." "Telephones are a complete waste of money and we won't ever use one, that's why." "Oh! Baloney," she shouted.

Mel looked at both of them, wide eyed, and crinkled nose, and thought, "who wouldn't want a phone?"

When they were finished eating, Katherine extended her hand to Mel and guided her to the bedroom's vanity. She pulled out the chair for Mel to sit, stood behind her, and loosened the lost girl's pigtails. "These hair ties are absolutely gorgeous and unusual. They are unlike anything I have seen in this area. Daisy, do you live in the city? Is that where your home is?"

Katherine formed two long braids going down the back of her head. Then she fetched two ribbons and tied a bow on each braid. She held up a gold and porcelain hand mirror for Mel to see the back of her head.

"What an old fashioned looking mirror, just like everything else in this house," Mel believed. She checked out her hair and parted her lips to form a slight smile, and Katherine took that as a sign of approval.

Finney had followed them into the bedroom and was lying on a rug next to the bed. "Finney, how do you like Daisy's braids?" She rose from the rug, happy to hear her name being called, and jumped up onto Katherine to plant a big wet kiss on her face. Katherine laughed and nudged the dog back down. When they got up to leave, Finney joined them.

"Let's go upstairs to the loft, where you can have some quiet time, Daisy." Katherine placed her hand on Mel's back. "It's my sewing room, but I'll give you a quilt to lie on so you can rest there for a little while.

I'm sure Finney would love to take a nap next to you, if you don't mind." Mel nodded subtly as she looked up at her to let her know she was fine with that.

The sewing room was on the small side; enough space for a sewing machine and cabinet, a rocking chair, and a storage closet. It was in the front of the house and had one small window that let the slightest amount of light in. Finney plopped on the floor right where the beam of light shined. If Mel stood up on the chair, she'd be able to see out. But not now. She was too tired from the long walk that morning.

"Daisy, you did a very brave thing today by rescuing my husband. And to think, if he hadn't brought Finney along you may not have found him. We're extremely lucky you showed up when you did.

Do you remember how you got to the meadow?

Did someone bring you there?"

Katherine hoped for any clue at all. She tucked a blanket around the child and questioned further.

"Have you a sister, or a brother, maybe?"

Mel wasn't ready to share any details, for fear of being sent to the looney bin. Having no idea what tomorrow would bring; at this moment she felt safe with Katherine and Charles watching over her. Mel couldn't remember the last time anyone brushed her hair or tucked her into a bed. Or, served her two helpings of soup. *They must be good people.*

After Katherine went back downstairs, Mel pulled the treasured stone out of her pocket and studied it for a moment, then ran her fingers over a faint etching on the stone's bottom. She considered hiding it somewhere in the room, but decided to keep it with her instead. A few minutes later, the lost girl and the dog were fast asleep.

The sheriff arrived soon after and the three adults chatted about the unusual event of the morning. Sheriff Nelson told them there were no calls about a missing girl as yet and that he'd go down to the local paper and have them print an urgent notice to run in the morning news.

"I'll need a good description of her." He pulled out a pad and a pen. Charles spoke first. "She's about 11 or 12 based on her height. I'd say she's 4-1/2 feet tall, but I can give you a more accurate measure after she wakes up. And average weight or somewhat bony."

"She has a tanned complexion and lovely caramel hair that reaches her waist." Katherine continued. "Oh! And two distinct eye colors. Blue and brown."

"Does she have any birthmarks or scars that you saw?" Asked the sheriff. "Not that I noticed," replied Katherine. "Okay. That's a good start. Call me if there's anything else you can think of." Katherine replied in a sarcastic tone. "We'll have to run down to the pay phone because Charles here doesn't see any reason we should own a phone."

Charles ignored Katherine's dig about modern conveniences and guided the sheriff to the door.

After several hours of a peaceful sleep, Mel's eyes darted around the dimly lit room. Startled at the unfamiliar space surrounding her, she cried out. "MAMA!"

A few minutes later, at the sound of footsteps approaching, she clenched her blanket and crab crawled to the furthest corner of the room. Worried eyes fixed at the doorway.

When Mel saw Katherine enter the room, she casually relaxed her back against the wall. She shook her head and recalled the day's event that led her here. *How long was I sleeping?*

Katherine reached for Mel's hand. It was soft and damp. Katherine pulled her close to her side and gave her a comforting hug. "You're gonna be okay, sweet girl. Would you like to come downstairs now?"

Mel heard people talking in the living room and tried to eavesdrop. "Who's here?" "Oh, it's just Jim, the town sheriff. He's going to help us find your family. Would you like to meet him?" Mel shrugged her shoulders, and strained to listen to the conversation taking place between the men.

"I can take her over to the orphanage after she wakes up," said the sheriff. "Or she can stay here for the time being if you don't mind the added responsibility."

"Oh, it won't be necessary to take her to an orphanage, sheriff. She's been no trouble, and we have the room. It's the least I can do for the person who saved my life today."

"Alright then." Replied Jim. "You know where to find me if anything changes. Oh, and I'll have the misses send over some of Stephanie's old clothes for the girl." "We'd appreciate that. Thanks, Jim."

"Good." Mel felt relieved upon hearing she'd be staying here with the Wilhelms while they searched for her mother. The thought of that strange, grungy man discovering her once more was unbearable.

After the sheriff left, Mel followed Katherine to the stairs. When she landed on the bottom step, she spied Charles sitting in a chair by the window, reading a newspaper, and she noticed the strangest thing.

The headline read: U.S. President Harding introduces the first radio into the White House. *President Harding? NO. The President IS Nixon.*

She thought back to when Mrs. Bartlett taught the class a song to help them memorize the order of presidents. She remembered a president Harding. Mel tried singing the song in her head, counting each one on her fingers. It was no use though, because she'd forgotten most of it.

Another headline read: Grand Opening of the Rivoli Theatre. Rutherford's first Vaudeville show sells out as hundreds of Rutherfordians and out of towners show up for opening night.

Opening night? That theater's been open many years. I remember watching Mary Poppins there when I was seven or eight. Something strange is going on here.

Th̲e R̲ealization

The Wilhelms agreed to let Mel spend the night. And, when the next day came and there was no inquiry, she remained there.

Days passed, then weeks.

There was never any inquiry as to the lost girl, so the Wilhelms continued to care for her as if she was their own daughter. Still, they knew nothing more about her than they did the day they met.

They anticipated her parents would show up, eventually. Mel had her doubts though. She reasoned that if the year was indeed 1922, as claimed in the newspaper, her mother couldn't have come to get her.

This is confusing and illogical. But it would undoubtedly account for the peculiar attire and the absence of a telephone or television in the residence.

Daisy wondered if she could be delirious.

It was time to record her first entry in the diary Katherine gave her to write down private thoughts.

Or secrets, she considered. Mel opened her wardrobe and pulled out the diary she had stashed in the bottom corner under her secret stone.

May 2, 1922

Dear Diary,

Katherine gave this to me yesterday.
She thought it would help if I wrote down
my feelings. I'll wear the key on a string
around my neck at all times, to prevent
people from opening the lock and snooping.
Soon I must figure out how I ended up in
1922... Unless, I'm actually dead. Who knows?
This whole thing is all VERY weird.
I haven't told anyone my real name yet.
They just call me Daisy so I guess I'll go by
that now.
PS. I wonder about my mom Charla a lot.
As mean as she was, I do miss her.
I wonder if she misses me?

Daisy

Six

SUMMER 1922

GRACE

Squealing with excitement at the news of voyaging to America on a steamship, 11-year-old Grace did spins around the room. She rocked back and forth, mimicking rough seas, and drove her parents crazy with her overzealous nature.

Grace was all ears as her stuffy father proudly shared all the particulars of their move to America. "Only affluent people could afford the luxury of transatlantic passage." Huxley bragged in a patronizing tone. "As one of the largest investors of a new riverfront vacation resort, I'll make sure everyday living will be like a holiday for us."

His cigar dangled between two fingers. He blew out a puff of smoke before placing it to rest in the big crystal ashtray on the desk.

When Huxley told a story, it was always as if he was giving a presentation on stage. "America is the land of opportunity, Gracie." He opened his arms wide, as if to demonstrate something huge. "You, my darling, will receive the finest education and therefore achieve great success in all you strive for."

Grace loved her father. He worked a lot and was rarely home, so she appreciated the attention. But she was only eleven years and old had no immediate aspirations at the moment. "Boring!" She thought as she yawned.

"Father, can we please get a puppy when we get to America?"

Huxley walked over to his daughter and led her to sit on the Davenport sofa in front of the fireplace. He sat in the armchair across from her.

"We'll leave at the end of this month, after your school year is finished. That should give you enough time to say goodbye to your friends and help your mum with the packing."

He removed a small notebook and pen from his shirt pocket and started writing. "Your toothbrush and powder, jam-jams, bath slippers, and robe, can go in your canvas bag. All other items of clothing shall go in the trunk. Understand?" "Yes, father."

"Help your little brother with his packing, as well. Here, take this list so you remember."

"But we're not leaving for weeks!" Grace exclaimed as she eyeballed the list.

"It's good to be organized and prepared," he advised.

"Okay." Her head drooped. She visualized saying goodbye to her friends and the only home she'd ever known.

"And we'll see about that puppy when we're in America," he added. Grace perked up and gave him a slight smile before sliding off the sofa and finding her way out of the room.

8 DAYS AFTER SEA VOYAGE

Not all immigrants who sailed into New York had to go through Ellis Island, the traditional port of entry. First- and second-class passengers submitted to a brief shipboard inspection and then disembarked at the piers in New York or New Jersey, where they passed through customs.

People in third class, though, were transported to the giant Customs Hall on Ellis Island. While there, they underwent medical and legal inspections to ensure that they didn't have a contagious disease, or some condition that would make them a burden to the government.

Grace and her family disembarked with the upper class passengers at the Port of New York. They hailed a cab to the luxurious Biltmore Hotel in midtown Manhattan, where they'd spend a short time exploring the sites, before settling into their new home in New Jersey.

They visited Carnegie Hall to see a very entertaining Charlie Chaplin film. And also spent a day at the Coney

Island Amusement Park riding the carousel and the ferris wheel. And tasting American treats like nickel red hots, cotton candy and root beer.

On the last day in New York Mr. & Mrs. Dalton promised the children a trip to Macy's. The world's largest department store that spanned an entire city block. Shopping was a treat for them and they were very excited about making a purchase of their choice.

Grace chose a pair of patent leather Mary Jane pumps and six-year-old Thomas chose a Tinker construction kit. Elizabeth bought a new pair of T-strap shoes with high hopes there would be dancing in their new town. And Charles purchased a pocket watch.

The next day, the family traveled by rail to their new home in Rutherford, where Grace, a social butterfly, was anxious to make new friends.

Seven

DAISY & GRACE
A NEW SCHOOL

Three weeks had passed since the first day Daisy came to live with the Wilhelms and they knew little about her. "She's twelve years old, and stubborn, is as much as we know about our guest." Katherine told Charles. "I agree. It's time to sit her down and find out exactly who she is."

They started with a simple question.

"Daisy, when is your birthday?" —

"April 8th." "Oh! Darn. We just missed it. I would have loved to host a party for you." Charles chimed in. "Katherine bakes the world's most delicious strawberry cupcakes with fresh cream topping." Katherine smiled at her husband. "I'll bake the cupcakes anyway!"

Daisy thought back to the party she was supposed to have for her last birthday. Anger filled her bones and her face got heated. She hated her mother for that.

"Is everything alright Daisy? We don't have to have a party if you don't want one." Daisy shrugged her shoulders and turned her head to the side. "Okay, well why don't we think about it for a few days, hmm?" Asked Katherine before continuing with her prepared pep talk.

"Daisy, we've discussed your progress since you've been here, and we both feel that you're ready to start school. Nevertheless, since it's the end of the school year, we think it'll be alright if you wait until September. Then you can start at the beginning of the year, just like the other children.

I imagine you've been to school before, yes?" Daisy (she was getting used to her new name) nodded.

"Do you remember what grade you were in before you came to live with us?" "6th grade." "Okay. And your grades? Were you a good student?" Asked Katherine. Daisy smiled and shook her head yes then added, "I was often chosen to be the teacher's helper."

"Now we're getting somewhere." Katherine thought. And, Charles had a slick idea. "I bet your teacher, Mrs.—" He paused and waited for Daisy to offer the teacher's name. "Mrs. Bartlett." "Right, Mrs. Bartlett. I bet you were one of her favorites?" Daisy shrugged her shoulders.

The Wilhelms kept their meeting brief since they were hesitant to press Daisy with too many questions.

When they were finished talking Charles announced that he had an errand to run. He opened the money tin on the kitchen shelf and grabbed a handful of pennies, then left the house. He went directly to the only payphone in town, located in front of the police station. He picked up the handset and asked the operator to be connected to every local school.

He was certain this would help them find Daisy's family. But after dozens of calls to elementary and middle schools in the area, he had no luck finding a teacher named Mrs. Bartlett. He'd have to try schools farther away, but that would require paying for a long distance call which was just was too expensive.

He saw Officer Nelson coming out of the corner store

and waved him over. "Hi Jim." "Oh hey there Charles. How's everything going with your house guest?" "She's settling in real nice, getting more comfortable and trusting.

Where she came from and how she got here is all still a big puzzle, but we learned some new information today that gives us hope."

Charles explained everything they learned and then explained how he made dozens of calls to the local schools looking for her teacher. He asked Officer Nelson if his department could take on the expense of making long distance calls to schools outside the county. "We can certainly do that Charles. Smart thinking on your part. I'll add this to our administrative task list and as soon as I know something I'll deliver the news in person. It may take a few days though." "Thanks Jim, sounds good."

Two days later Officer Nelson paid a visit to the Wilhelm's house to deliver the news.

"Sorry, Charles. We called the New Jersey Board of Education, and there weren't any records of a teacher named Bartlett. Are you sure that's the correct name?" "I'm certain that's the name she gave us." "Interesting. Okay, then. We'll have to figure out another way to investigate this." Officer Jim tipped his hat. "If there's anything else, you know where to find me."

Grace was more than ready for her first day of school. She had been in her new town for two long weeks and was becoming antsy with the anticipation of making American friends. She put on her new dress, a light blue gingham with a frilly collar, and carefully laced her black and white boots.

Downstairs in the kitchen, Elizabeth Dalton was preparing lunch baskets for Grace and Grace's younger brother, Thomas. She placed a jelly sandwich and an apple into each one before the three of them headed out the door for the short walk to their new school.

"Wait! Mother. Shouldn't we say goodbye to father before we go?" Grace inquired. Elizabeth chuckled. "Oh darling, he's gone off to work already. We'll see him at supper, and then you can tell him all about your first day." Grace was used to her father's early and late work hours, so this wasn't a surprise.

The school was a two-story red brick building with a large entry landing at the main entrance and four tall pillars going up to the base of the gable. The building had two wings on either side. One was for the boys to enter and the other for the girls.

"Mother, I couldn't possibly be more excited at this very moment. How could I? It's been a dreadfully long summer waiting for this day, and it's finally come. Imagine in just a matter of moments I will walk through that door and meet my new American friends." Elizabeth felt relieved. She knew the move was difficult for Grace.

"I hope it's all you've dreamed of, my dear. But first we must go to the registrar's office. So take my hand, both of you, and off we'll go to get you enrolled."

As they sat on the bench in the hallway near the girls' entrance, waiting for new student registration forms, the school bell rang and children filed in through the doors.

Grace's eyes scanned the corridor, watching the other girls closely; they were talking and giggling amongst themselves. Some carried a lunch basket like hers, and some carried a book. One girl, who looked about the same age, but taller, wearing two long golden braids behind her head, gave a slight wave of hello as she passed.

"Did you see that girl, mother? Someone waved to me. Her eyes were striking. Did you see? And two different colors!" "Well, isn't that unusual."

"Mother, are my eyes two different colors?" Asked Thomas. "No, of course not, dear. You know you have two hazel colored eyes, silly." "Thomas, why must you copy everything?" Grace rolled her eyes.

Later that day, after lunch, Grace went outside to the playground. She watched Thomas and some other boys on the swings for a few minutes. Pumping their legs back and forth in a friendly competition to see who's swing would go higher. She glanced over to see Daisy sitting under a beautiful oak tree and decided to go introduce herself.

"Hi! I'm Grace. Today's my first day." Grace waved enthusiastically. Daisy's eyes went directly to the blond streak in Grace's chestnut brown hair. "It's a type of birthmark," uttered Grace. "Oooh. Hi, I'm Daisy. I'm new too." Grace replied in a humorous tone, "well we have one thing in common so far."

"Somehow I can tell we're gonna be good friends," blurted Daisy. She stood up and gave Grace a slight hug. "You'll see. I like your accent. It reminds me of someone I used to know."

Daisy's former teacher, Mrs. Bartlett, was from England, and she instantly recognized Grace's accent. Hearing her pronunciation of words stirred up some memories, but at the same time it was a comfort. Daisy loved Mrs. Bartlett and wondered if she'd ever see her again.

September 8, 1922

Dear Diary,
My first week of 7th grade was better than expected. I've already made friends with Grace, who's new to the area from England. She speaks with a British accent, like Mrs. Bartlett. And she has the most unusual streak in her hair, which she refers to as a birthmark.

I think we're going to be lifelong friends.
I HOPE SO ANYWAY!

And, I really like Union School.

Daisy

For their entire first year in Rutherford, the girls kept the same routine. After school they'd walk to Grace's house, and always shuffling behind them was her little brother Thomas, kicking up pebbles from the gravelly path while he tried to keep the pace.

A wealthy family, the Daltons, lived in a three-story Victorian style home with a wrap around front porch and a tall bay window that allowed a clear view of the river from the double parlor on the main floor. The wood exterior was dark red and featured a stone chimney running up the side.

The house was significantly larger than the riverfront cottage where Daisy lived. It had two sets of stairs. The girls would spend hours running up one staircase and down the other, often playing hiding games with Thomas. There were too many hiding places to count, but Thomas could find them when he persisted.

It was a game they'd play until he was old enough not to care where the girls were. And that was fine with them.

When they weren't playing tricks on Thomas, they read fashion magazines, or shared secrets. Daisy came close to blurting out her secret more than once. But the fear of not knowing what Grace's reaction would be, stopped her from sharing.

Grace had a beautiful display of dolls that sat on a tall shelf in her bedroom. She was getting too old to play with them, but they were a part of her childhood and thought they earned the privilege to stay.

Daisy had no interest in dolls. That's where their personalities differed. She had been born with a natural curiosity and wanted to capture everything through the lens of a camera. She enjoyed being outdoors above all else.

After Charles bought Daisy her own Brownie Box camera you couldn't pay her to stay inside. She was always off on some type of photo excursion.

Across the street from the Dalton's house, and along the riverbank were woods, soon to be developed into riverfront vacation homes. Grace's father, a "white-collar worker" was one investor of the future community. It was a fast-growing town that attracted travelers from all over.

The construction of cottages for the "blue-collar workers" and their families, where Daisy lived, took place a few years earlier.

Charles Wilhelm strived to have his own successful photography business one day. Secured to the door leading into his basement darkroom was a reminder of his hopes and dreams:

BE MY OWN BOSS BY MY 40th BIRTHDAY

But until then, he'd continue working for the architectural firm as their photographer to document the development, for reports and publications.

EIGHT

SUMMER 1923
ONE YEAR LATER

July 12, 1923

Dear Diary,

My parents enrolled me in "Talk Therapy."
They think that a childhood incident is the
source of my emotional difficulties.
WELL YEA! If they had any notion of my
bizarre experience, they'd need therapy,
too.
I'm happy to say my last humdrum session
with Dr. Klein was today.
We talked about the most ridiculous things
and nothing truly significant. One thing we
never discussed was my past.
I wasn't sure whether I could trust him with

----> continued

my secret so I never mentioned it.

I'll confide in someone once I've worked up the courage and I hope that day comes soon; otherwise, I feel like my head will explode trying to keep this information to myself.

The good news, besides the fact that I'm not going back, was the Doctor's diagnosis. He concluded that I am merely a storyteller who will make a brilliant author one day.

He told Katherine and Charles I am a typical teenager with an active imagination who's hit all her age-related targets.

Daisy

✦

Memories of Daisy's former life were fading. But the recollection of the horrible man with the smelly hands from the zoo still lingered in her mind.

Every so often she'd have a flash of her mother Charla, and the worn down apartment the two lived in. Memories of coming home to the empty space and preparing a jelly sandwich for dinner, or finding empty whiskey bottles in the kitchen. She didn't really miss any of it.

Her mother wasn't a loving type person. More of a guardian who's only job was to put a roof over her daughter's head and stock the cabinets with basic food staples.

After Daisy spent time living with the Wilhelms, she realized what little effort her mother Charla put into parenting.

Daisy was an only child, and all she knew about her father was that he had a bad temper and other habits that were unfit for raising a child. Charla told her they were better off without a dirt bag like him around.

Daisy hadn't seen him since she was a year old and had no recollection of what he looked like, and hoped she'd meet him again one day, so she could form her own opinion of him.

～

Grace pulled the handle on the screen door, and as per usual, Finney came running as soon as she heard the screech. Grace bent down to pet the family canine before she walked into the cottage.

"Daisy! I'm here." "Okay, be right down." Grace looked around the room while she waited.

Mr. Wilhelm's black & white framed photos on the walls told the family's story.—

Katherine & Charles' wedding.

A small child sitting on a pony.

Daisy standing next to Finney.

A lilac bush in the river's foreground.

"I've never seen these photos before. Someone hung them recently," thought Grace. Katherine came in from the backyard. "I thought I heard your voice, Grace. Aren't the photos beautiful?"

Daisy thumped down the stairs. "I'm ready to go!"

"Alright girls. Before you go riding off into the wilderness, there are some rules to follow." Both girls, wide eyed, stared at Katherine obediently.

There's an area about four miles away from here that's off limits. "You know where the meadow is that's on the north side of River Street. We've driven past it many times." Both girls shook their heads, yes.

"On the other side of the meadow is a forest, and beyond that is a Native American burial site. It's considered very sacred and we want to respect that." "Is it a cemetery?" Asked Daisy. "I'm not quite sure," replied Katherine. "Just stay away from it." The girls eyeballed each other. "Okay."

Outside, the girls got onto their bikes. Daisy pushed the middle of her skirt between her legs until it resembled long shorts. She hated always having to wear a dress. "So ridiculous," she mumbled. "What is?" Asked Grace. "Wearing a dress all the time. Girls should be allowed to wear pants." "Hmmm. I'd never thought about that. I like the idea!"

"So, where do you want to go?" "Let's ride to the playground and see what the daily activity is." "I heard they were making pressed flower cards today. My neighbor, Mrs. Garrett, is giving the class, that's how I know." "Sounds fun," replied Daisy.

"Also, I want to stop in the fabric store later to see if the new samples came in." "You're really becoming quite the seamstress, Grace, aren't you?" "It's become my passion, really. After I finish making the drapes for my bedroom I plan to learn upholstery so I can recover the chaise lounge by my window. Just wait until you see the peacock print I plan to use. The blue colors are breathtaking."

"Peacocks? No way! They give me nightmares." Daisy stated. "I hope you're joking. Nobody gets a nightmare from peacocks." "I do. And one day you'll learn why." "One day? Why not today?" Daisy ignored her question and pushed down faster on the peddle until she was half a block ahead. She stopped the bike and waited for Grace to catch up. Both girls took a break at the edge of the road under a shade tree.

"Can I ask you something, Grace?" "Of course. What is it?" "Have you ever heard the story about how the townspeople used to picnic out by that sacred site and then one day they all stopped going?"

"Daisy, you know I don't pay much attention to what goes on in this town. Especially rumors about what happened before I lived here." Daisy shook her head.

"The last time I was at the candy store I overheard that busybody Mrs. Clark telling a younger boy 'that children who go near that place disappear.' You should have seen the frightened look on his face before he bolted. And, did you hear Katherine today telling us not to go there? Something very mysterious is going on around here."

"I don't like to get mixed up in things that don't concern me," affirmed Grace. "Well I do, and I'm determined to learn more about it. When school starts back up in September I'm going to talk with the history teacher and see if he knows anything."

September 2, 1923

Dear Diary,

My family and I are in Lake Hopatcong for Labor Day Weekend. Charles wanted to take us on a mini vacation before school starts, so he rented a cabin here, one block from the lake.

I've met several friends, including a really cute boy named John who has two sisters close to my age. We all spent the entire day swimming at the lake today, and tonight some of the families are going to Bertrand Island Amusement Park.

I don't know what to expect when I get there. John explained that it's like a carnival, but I've never been to a carnival.

School starts in two days. 8th grade here I come.

Daisy

Nine

FALL 1923

RESEARCH

September 5, 1923

Dear Diary,

This week marks the return of school after the summer break.

I've been anxious to talk with Mr. Nast, the history teacher (a.k.a. Mr. Past, for obvious reasons) about the sacred site. The first opportunity I had was today, before last period.

I wanted to ask if he knew anything about the children who vanished from the infamous big wall there.

--------> continued

But the meeting didn't go as good as I had
hoped. He told me he didn't engage in gossip
and advised me to conduct my own
research at the library.
BRILLIANT idea, I thought.

In eight-grade English, we're composing short
stories, and the words from our new
vocabulary list HAVE TO be used.
ASTONISHING, is one of the words.
I immediately thought of writing about
how astonishing it was to crawl through a
wall, remove a mystical stone, and then
travel back in time 50 years. Seriously!

I should definitely not mention that on the
essay I turn in, for fear It might earn me a
free stay at the looney bin, or worse, a
research lab.

<u>Daisy</u>

A week passed since the start of school, and Mr.
Nast's suggestion of going to the library for re-
search weighed on Daisy's mind. She made a list
of questions she wanted answers for;
- *Did Native Americans have special traits?*
- *Was the architecture of the wall specific to any rituals?*

- *What about the hollow opening inside of the wall?*
  Was that used as a safe keeping space for artifacts?
- *And what would explain the stone I found?*
- *What caused the stone to sparkle?*

No one was willing to respond to her exhausting number of queries and she hoped she'd find some answers at the library.

September 13th, 1923

Dear Diary,

I've always loved doing research, so I look forward to the Friday's that Katherine takes me to the library, which typically occurs every two weeks.

My latest interest is that sacred burial site where the children disappeared.

I find it quite odd that NO ONE will TALK ABOUT IT!

Daisy

Daisy looked forward to fact-finding Fridays at the library. She researched everything from photography to gemstones, and more recently, ancient Native American traits and rituals.

Her interest in the library actually started when Charles gave her a big clunky Brownie Box camera. She wanted to learn more about this ancient device and compare it to the Kodak Instamatic Mrs. Baldwin had.

Unfortunately, there was no such information on the Instamatic available. Instead, she studied lighting techniques and photo developing until she became quite the expert photographer for a 13-year-old.

She carried that big box camera with her everywhere. As a member of the Brownie Camera Club, she was eligible to win contest prizes should she ever have a first place photo. Now she had to think of something to shoot that would be prize worthy.

She took photos of Grace in her long floral skirt sitting by a river flooded with reflections, and captured Finney jumping high into the air to catch a ball, and so many others.

Nevertheless, after learning about the sacred burial location outside of town through local rumor, her mind started to race with possibilities. She consequently became interested in Native American culture. She wanted to learn everything she could about the area and the giant wall, which she was positive she'd seen before.

She opened up the card catalog to S and flipped through the index cards until she found one titled Sacred Sites Native American. She noted the titles of several books related to caves and mounds, and a few with maps, and then devoted an hour to perusing page after page from each.

"Can you make a photocopy of this, please?" She held up the page with the map of NJ for the librarian to see. The lady reflected on the question and then asked if Daisy could repeat what she said. "I'd like a photocopy of this map, please." Daisy grew impatient. "Don't you have a Xerox machine?"

"I'm sorry, I don't know what that is."

"Oh, forget it! May I have a paper and pencil please? I'll draw a copy myself."

Startled at the child's abruptness, the librarian with her uptight mouth made a face and pointed to the counter across the room.

⌒℮⌒

In the car on the way home, Daisy asked Katherine for more details about the sacred site. "You are the most persistent child I have ever known." Daisy raised her eyebrow.

"Here's what I know, and please let this be the end of the inquiries." *I'm listening.* Daisy thought, as she turned to face Katherine.

"Native Americans lived in this area for hundreds of years before we arrived. They built a very large wall around the site to conceal secret ceremonies. The townspeople believe they possessed extraordinary traits which were passed down to their ancestors for generations."

"What are extraordinary traits?" Asked Daisy. Katherine ignored her and continued. "Their village was in Waterloo, which is now a preservation site that is off limits to everyone.

About ten years ago, several teenage boys disappeared, and some believe that they had been at that sacred site." Katherine continued. "Those boys never returned."

Daisy was just about to interrupt her mother, but stopped herself. "For those reasons, we ask that you do not go near there. And stop asking endless questions about it."

Daisy was agonizing over the details. It was a lot of

information to absorb. *I need to see Grace asap.*

"You never mentioned those boys before. Did you know them?" Asked Daisy. Katherine faced her daughter, "We weren't living here at the time, so no. But I heard their families searched for them for years."

"Can you drive me to Grace's house? I can walk home from there."

Later that night, Daisy made a diary entry.

September 14, 1923

Dear Diary,

I can't quit wondering about the old sacred burial site and what occurs there that everyone is so terrified of?
If children genuinely disappeared from there, where did they go?
Grace finds it odd that I constantly bring it up. But what she doesn't know, is that something similar happened to me.
   When I ask Katherine about the rumors she gets anxious. I wonder if she knows more than she's letting on.

Daisy

TEN

SUMMER 1924

A SECRET EXPLORATION

Everyone in town knew Daisy. The child from no-where who just showed up one day and saved Charles' life. That event made her a really big deal.

A pleasant child, she had come out of her shell, but it took a few years. She always waved hello when she zoomed by on her old hand-me-down bicycle. That stuffed bear of hers, the one she received from the Wilhelms when she was formally adopted, always had the front-row seat in the basket attached to the handlebars.

If she wasn't at the library with her nose in a book, she was off on some adventure going God knows where in a hurry.

She wore her long caramel hair in two braids behind her neck, and they reached half way down her back. She cared little for the 1920s style waves or ringlets or anything that required fussing. She was a friendly, but peculiar child with a sparkle in her blue and brown eyes. She, without a doubt, gave the townspeople a lot to talk about.

Now, the 2nd week of June and the end of the school year was on this very day. Standing at the front of her 8th-grade classroom next to her desk trying to finish up one last lesson, the teacher paused. Knowing her students were distracted by the excitement of summer break, she gave in and closed her book.

"Okay then, we have 10 minutes before the bell rings. Who wants to tell me what they'll be doing over the holiday?" A dozen hands went up and there was lots of chatter and squirming around in seats.

Grace was just about to stick her arm up when Daisy clenched it. "Noooo! You can't be spilling our secrets to the whole class, silly." Daisy seemed bossy to an unusual extent, which inspired the snarky response from her best friend. "Oops. Sorry." She rolled her eyes.

Annoyed at her friend's complacent attitude, Daisy spoke with impatience. "I've explained this to you. This plan is very important to my photography hobby, but you know we cannot tell anyone where we're going. If my parents find out they'll send me away to summer camp. Do you agree not to tell anyone?"

In her most sincere tone, Grace whispered, "Yes." Then they locked pinkies.

The teacher dismissed the class for the last time and, since Grace and Daisy sat in the back, they were the first ones out the door and their classmates all stampeded out behind them.

Walking down the steps of the school, Daisy noticed a change in Grace's attitude. "What's wrong Grace? You seem blasé." "I guess I am." When I almost told the class about the trip, I realized we're really going through with this. And now I'm having second thoughts."

Daisy's eyes drifted toward Al Gibson, the boy who flirted with her when she shopped at the candy store his parents owned. He was really cute, but she had no time for boys right now.

"Hello! Daisy, are you listening?" "Yes, sorry." "Look, Daisy. I think I'm having second thoughts about going tomorrow. I feel bad about sneaking around and lying to my parents. I'm not as plucky as you." "Plucky?" Daisy laughed at the phrase. "I just think if our parents forbid us from going there, they must have a good reason."

Daisy didn't know what to say after hearing her confession. She just stood there with her fists clenched at her side, glaring at her friend. "Grace, you've been my constant friend. We've been planning this for a while and now you tell me?"

"I was excited when we were planning it out, but now that the time has come, my stomach is twitchy and I get scared at the thought of it all."

Daisy, not one to stay mad, eased her posture and tried to lighten the current mood. "Well, getting twitchy, whatever that means, sounds made up."

One long, silent minute passed before Daisy added. "Just kidding, dork! Do you think I'm not positively anxious as well? We've got to do this. I'll be really bummed if you don't come with me."

Grace scrunched her nose and repeated, "bummed, dork? What kind of words are those?"

Daisy shook her head, and continued walking down the schoolyard path that met the street. *I've got to convince her to come with me tomorrow.*

Thomas caught up to the girls, and the three walked in silence for 20 minutes. Kicking pebbles as usual, he didn't notice the lack of conversation between the two girls.

When they reached Riverside Drive, Daisy, not in any mood for more shilly-shally, decided today she would go directly home instead of sticking to her usual routine, which was going to Grace's house to play before she went home for supper.

She made an intentional turn in the other direction. Then, having no regard for Grace's reluctance for going on their excursion, she confirmed the original plan. "I'll meet you at the corner in front of the paper mill at 8am if you change your mind. Don't be late." Daisy's irritation was evident to Grace. "Just quit being so salty. I'll be there."

June 12, 1924

Dear Diary,

I've learned a lot about Native American
rituals and their heritage.
It's very interesting, in fact. These
Indigenous people have reportedly
inherited gifts of all kinds, and the time
travel gene is one such example.
What I need to figure out is if the wall was
used as a portal for traveling.
And what if it STILL is??? That could help
to EXPLAIN WHAT HAPPENED TO ME. And
perhaps those boys who disappeared.
YET WHY? And HOW?

I also gained some knowledge about the
stone I discovered. I need to return to the
wall and survey the area.

Grace trusts I'm going to take photos, and I
wish I could tell her everything, but I still
think it's too soon. If I ever have solid proof,
then I might reveal the truth.

Daisy

Daisy's weakness was fighting the impulse to do something she shouldn't. No longer the shy, sweet little girl

who went along with everything. She had little fear and rarely got that twitchy feeling in the gut, like others talked about. It just didn't happen.

Daisy loved a challenge and trusted her sixth sense, which was something she always had. She just didn't tap into it on that fateful day at the animal sanctuary. But perhaps she wasn't meant to do so.

Today, the first day of the summer holiday, was the day she would go against Katherine's warnings to never - ever - go anywhere near the old sacred site.

"I'm 14 years old, practically an adult," she mumbled to Finney, while she patted her furry coat. Daisy glanced at the clock and saw that it was almost time to meet Grace. "Oops, Finney, I've got to run." She jumped up and licked Daisy's face. "You be a good girl and we'll play catch later."

Daisy stepped into her jumpsuit, laced up her shoes and grabbed her camera case and a map before heading downstairs and out the door at an accelerated pace.

The screen door creaked as it came to a slamming close. "Daisy!" Called Katherine from the window. "Don't be gone long, you have chores to do." "I know, I won't." Daisy picked up her bicycle from where it leaned against the house and waved goodbye.

"Right on time." Daisy called out to Grace as she pulled up on her Colson Fairy bike. "Figures you'd outdo me, again." They both laughed. Grace couldn't help it if her family had tons more money than her friend's family and just about everything she owned was nicer and newer than Daisy's.

"Let's skedaddle before someone sees us." They jumped on their bikes, with Daisy taking the lead, and gave a quick wave as they passed a group of local boys who were up early and skipping rocks into the river. "I wonder if Al is over there?" Grace asked sarcastically. Daisy shrugged her shoulders and pedaled faster. "No time for boys."

It was a quick ride on a packed down gravel road, like most of the roads in Rutherford, and Daisy had to put her foot down several times to keep herself from sliding. Her old bike was a little less dependable than Grace's, but she managed just fine despite her almost slip-ups. The road crunched under their tires as they sped along, keeping a steady pace.

Grace shouted to the back of Daisy's head. "The morning sounds are my favorite! The birds singing and calling out to their friends, the sound the leaves make when the tree branches sway back and forth. It's so peaceful out here in the early morning."

"You're such a dork," replied Daisy in sarcasm as she turned to look at Grace. "Today my favorite sound will be the crinkling noise this old map makes when I unfold it." She pulled the map from the basket and waved it back and forth as she continued pedaling.

When the good road ended and the worn out trail began, Daisy came to an abrupt stop. She tipped her bike to the ground and motioned for Grace to do the same.

"Where'd you get that old map?" "I found it last year at the trading store. You know how my curiosity gets the best of me? I went back the next day with three eggs and I traded for it." She was proud of her bartering skill.

"It's a map of the entire park and the sacred wall. I've kept it hidden, tucked away behind the books on my bedroom shelf. It's way more detailed than the one I saw in the library." Grace was impressed by how thoroughly this trip had been planned.

"According to the map, the sacred wall is about an acre wide and is just past the meadow and the live oak trees. It looks like the trees surround a lush field of shrubs and grass. I'm not sure how it looks nowadays. But that's what it looked like when the map was produced."

Daisy picked up a stick and dragged it around on the ground, indicating what they'd potentially find when they reached the location. "If I'm reading this map correctly, we only have a mile further to go, but we'll have to leave the bicycles here." Daisy leaned hers up against a tree and gestured for Grace to follow.

"Grace, I'm pleased you came with me today. I know we'll be best friends forever after this." Daisy kicked some rocks out of her path and bent down to pick a wildflower to stick in her hair.

"There will be plenty of time for boys and other things when we're older, as my mother says. For now we should have fun being kids, explore all there is to explore, do the unimaginable, and take prize winning photos."

About a mile into their walk, Grace confessed her anxiety about going any further. "Daisy, you know I couldn't ask for a better friend than you, and I do love our secret adventures, but like I mentioned yesterday, I have concerns about going to the sacred wall.

There's also something I haven't told you that's adding to my angst." "What? What is it?" Questioned Daisy.

"Yesterday after you went home instead of coming over to my house, I went to the kitchen for a sticky bun like we always do after school. I heard the cook, Gertie, speaking to someone, so I stopped in the hall and stood to listen. It was Hank the grocer who came by with a delivery. I think he fancies her. She told me he always adds something special to the bags just for her.

Anyway, they stood talking for a while like they always do, but yesterday they were talking about those boys who disappeared all those years ago. You remember that story?" *Yea, I remember that story, that's why I'm here!* Daisy thought to herself.

"Hank mentioned, tomorrow (which is today) was the 10th anniversary of that dreadful day. And then Gertie said those two Harris brothers were always looking for some kind of trouble to get into, and it did not surprise her when they went missing. But dragging Walter into their trouble-making ways was unforgivable." Grace added. "Then, Hank added, I'm sorry about your nephew Gertie. The whole town still hopes he'll return one day." Daisy looked shocked.

"Whoa! Gertie's nephew was one of the boys who went missing?" "Yes." Replied Grace. "And then I remembered my mother talking about the rumors and the town gossip about those boys being out near the burial grounds and that they found evidence of it. She told me us children didn't need to know the details of it all." "My mother told me the same thing."

Daisy changed the subject. "You know I want to capture a prize winning photo. Besides that, I have a personal reason for needing to go there." "Oh?" Grace beamed with curiosity. "It's something I have a feeling deep down in my gut about, and I could be wrong, but I need to at least check into it. I want to tell you more, but not today. For now, please just trust me."

Grace took all this in. She put her head down and looked away. "Please don't be mad, Daisy, but I've decided not to go any further." She looked back up and straight at Daisy. Her lips quivering. "I'll wait for you here, okay? And please be careful." "That's okay, I get it. Maybe next time."

∞

Grace waved goodbye and then hiked around the area for a little while, admiring the vivid display of scattered flowers. Yellow dandelion, and daffodils that look like little trumpets, deep-purple meadow violets, tulips in orange, red, and white, and wild geranium.

Honey bees hunting for pollen could be heard in the distance.

She enjoyed the sounds of nature, including the chirping of the birds.

Grace was no longer anxious and was glad about her decision to not continue any further. Even if Daisy was annoyed with her, it didn't matter. She knew her best friend would get over it.

The soft green grass invited her to lie down. She closed her eyes and let the heat of the sun shining on her face hypnotize her into a deep sleep.

Some time later Grace was awakened by a sudden gust of wind, and unsure of how much time had passed she jumped to her feet.

It took her a minute to realize where she was.

She remembered Daisy continuing on without her to find the sacred site on foot.

"We laid the bikes down before Daisy took off. But where exactly was that?" Grace remembered passing a field of grass covered in dandelions near a clearing of trees.

"Somewhere near this area", she thought, but she wasn't sure how far she had wandered off.

"Where are the bicycles? What if I can't find them? I don't know my way back home. DAISSSSY!"

She called out a second time, but the only response she heard was her echo.

Worry starting creeping up inside her. She could feel the heat of panic running through her legs and straight up to her chest. The place where they left the bikes was her marker. She'd have no idea how to get back home unless she started at that point and backtracked.

"I'm lost, oh nooo. "Grace, pull yourself together." She imagined Daisy shouting in her ear. "There is no time for self-talk that is negative."

"I better make haste." Grace wasn't used to being out this way, let alone by herself. She walked at a fairly quick pace in search of the bikes, and after what seemed like forever, she wondered if she was going around in circles.

Just then, as if by the miracle of a guardian angel, a ray of sun shined through the opening between the trees right onto her Fairy bike, and her hopes soared. Breathing a big sigh of relief, Grace picked up her bike and hugged it.

However, there was still one lingering problem.

It looked like Daisy hadn't returned yet. Her bike was there, and the stuffed bear that went everywhere with Daisy had fallen out of the basket and was on the ground.

"Daisy, why are you taking so long to get back? She called out again. "DAISSSSY!"

Grace paced around nervously, wondering if she should wait longer. She had no idea of the time and getting lost in the dark crossed her mind more than once.

When there was no sign of her adventurous friend she picked up the teddy bear and peddled her bike back to town.

ELEVEN

WHERE'S DAISY?

Grace rode up the slope to her house at precisely the wrong time. Several neighbors were outside sitting in their yard chairs, sipping lemonade and watching their children play. If they didn't have anything to gossip about before, now they would. "Where have you been, young lady?" Elizabeth came charging toward her, arms flailing.

"The time slipped by so fast. I'm sorry, mother. Daisy and I rode our bikes to the park, and we lost track of time." She lied.

"Well, where is your adventurous friend, and why isn't she with you? Her mother came by earlier but I told her neither of you were here."

Elizabeth yelled out to Thomas to stay there with his friends until she got back. She took her daughter's hand, and pulled as she hurriedly headed toward the river to Daisy's house.

Grace was teary eyed and sniffling, not knowing where Daisy was or how she'd explain the situation to Mrs. Wilhelm. The stuffed bear tucked under her arm.

The screen door screeched as it opened in front of them. Mrs. Wilhelm, in one long drawn out sentence, uttered, "Elizabeth, how very nice to see you, Grace, you as well. Where is Daisy? Has something happened? I told that child not to be gone long. Grace, where is she?"

Grace knew she was in big trouble and the tears were now flowing like a faucet. "She wasn't with me since earlier today." Grace answered. "We went to the park, and when Daisy wanted to stay longer, I told her I was going home, and she didn't care. Said she'd stay there by herself." That was only half the truth, but after being pressured, she confessed the entire account.

When Daisy didn't return by nightfall, a search party was organized. And every day for the following weeks, one hundred people or more continued looking for Daisy. Her bicycle was found where Grace told them it would be. There was no other trace of her.

The Wilhelms hoped maybe her actual parents had found her and brought her home. Although this would be heart wrenching for Katherine and Charles, it was better than thinking something worse had happened.

Newspaper ads were placed for the missing teen, and the posters were hung around town. There were a few vigils held, and Daisy's family and friends clung to their hope of finding her unharmed.

By fall, the searches had long stopped.

The winter holidays came and went.

And then it was spring.

Daisy studied the old map she yanked from her pocket and followed it closely while walking a few hundred yards to where the burial ground should be, hoping nobody was watching.

According to this map, the sacred wall should be just past the live oak trees in a densely wooded area of a field.

She ventured down the old path that meandered through the woods. The abundance of trees, shrubs, and brush indicated that no new land development on this side of town had taken place. Still plenty of trees to climb, wildflowers to gather, chattering birds, and buzzing bees. She pinched another tiny flower from a bush and placed it in her hair next to the other one.

The moment Daisy reached the end of the path, the surroundings seemed familiar. *Had I been here before?* She could see up ahead a large stone circular wall sitting on top of a raised area, like the mounds she read about.

She stood still for a moment, took a quick glance about, and behind her, and when she was confident no one else was nearby, she walked cautiously up to the wall.

Incredible! I think this is the same location where I was taken captive two years ago.

The wall was shorter than she remembered, but in two years she hadn't yet grown tall enough to see over the edge. Daisy considered hoisting herself up to climb over, but instead walked along the outside of the wall until she reached the opening.

Thinking about the horrible day when she was dragged into the forest and restrained next to the wall caused her pulse to pound quicker than normal.

She could still remember the man's face and the stink from his hands.

It's crazy to think that all happened 50 years in the future. FIFTY YEARS!

I don't plan on crawling into any holes in the wall today!

Daisy stood in awe of the beautiful stones aligned in a spiral shape lining the wall's perimeter. She held up her camera and took several shots. Certain at least one would win a prize.

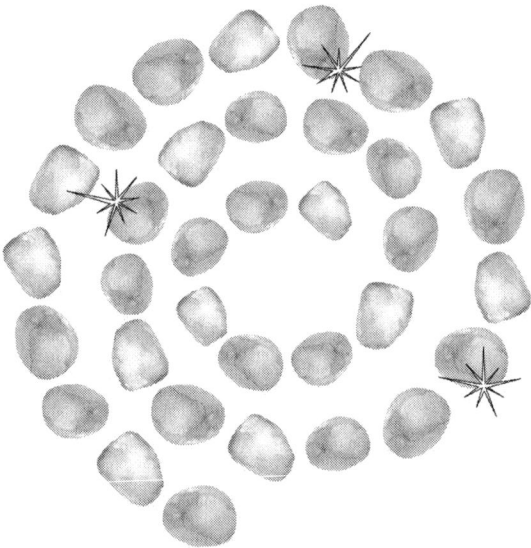

TWELVE

THE SPIRIT VISION
OF TRAVELS

E very stone was the shape of an egg, yet twice the size and different colors, mostly shades of blue or gray. Some were a reddish brown with speckles of gold. She had never seen more beautiful stones.

Well, maybe she had. The stone she kept hidden in her room, from the last time she was here, was just as beautiful, if not more so.

The structure of the wall, and the stones set perfectly in a spiral, looked like someone could have constructed it moments ago. Despite the fact that she knew the wall had to have been there for a hundred plus years, the construction and the way the stones were placed made it appear as though it had just been built.

How strange.

She inched her way closer for a better look but made sure not to get too close to the wall for fear of being swallowed up again. She stepped over the outer ring of rocks and most carefully picked up one of the gold speckled ones from the middle for closer examination. It was smooth and surprisingly warm to the touch, and on the underside was a faint shape carved out with a knife;

diagonal lines like a stretched out square and in the middle of the square was a small circle and three notches in the circle. *Interesting. I know I've seen these symbols before.*

Thinking back, Daisy remembered some books she had thumbed through in the apothecary store last year.

Hmmm, could this symbol be the spirit vision of travels? Did this have something to do with the tribe's extraordinary traits Katherine told her about?

She scratched her head and wished Katherine hadn't rushed her out the door that day before she sopped up more information. She loved anything out of the ordinary and for a 14-year-old was quite the visionary.

Staring down at the prized beauty in her hand, Daisy wondered if she should put it back or take it home to be with the other stone in her room. She cradled it with both hands and considered the idea.

Suddenly, her entire body and mind became intoxicated with an electric surge and she started to feel dizzy.

The gold specks that she was admiring minutes ago twinkled and sparked, as if they came to life.

A yellow, slightly transparent halo swirled around her hands as the rock began radiating heat. "Astonishing!" The swirling got bigger and bigger and took on the shape of a tornado. Startled, she let go of the rock.

THIRTEEN

WINTER 1949

WHAT HAVE I DONE?

urled up on the ground, under the vast protection of a live oak tree, and dressed only in her lightweight plaid jumpsuit, Daisy was shivering from the cold. She picked up her head "Ow!" And rubbed it where it had been lodged into the frosty November earth.

Alarmed at having no idea where she was or how she got there, she glanced around the area, grabbed hold of the camera that was still hanging around her neck, and tried to recall the earlier events. Her surroundings looked familiar, but felt unfamiliar at the same time.

Daisy's heart was racing pretty fast at this point and beads of sweat formed on her forehead despite the cold air. She looked up at the snowflakes falling from the sky.

What in the actual heck?

She recalled leaving her house in the morning, saying bye to Finney, riding bicycles through the woods, and reading an old map.

Is this a dream?

She shouted frantically into the woods. "GRACE! Where are you?"

She was really wracking her brain to recall anything more. Anything at all. She looked up to the sky, then she closed her eyes, and rubbed her forehead and took several deep cold breaths in the process. "I must go over all the details of the morning and think really hard;

It was the first day of summer break.

I left the house early to meet Grace.

We rode our bikes to the sacred shrine.

Yes! But Grace turned back.

I continued on by myself.

She wasn't with me when I discovered the wall.

Daisy's forehead wrinkled in relation to her busy mind. "Yes! I found the wall on the mound with beautiful stones in the middle."

It didn't matter when she spoke out loud. There wasn't a soul around to hear.

But... She wondered. *Where was the wall now? I know I made sure not to crawl into any holes this time. And the stone? What happened to you pretty little stone that I cradled in my hands just moments ago?*

Daisy looked around on the ground a bit and then, seemingly out of nowhere, an uninvited visitor showed up.

Officer Henry drove a newer model car that, when compared to automobiles in 1925, could give you the impression that the owner must be someone of grand status.

Still on the ground and feeling dazed, Daisy watched the automobile in the distance move slowly in her direction. It was quite fancy, a beautiful color of blue and like no car she'd seen in recent years.

"Who's this now? Must be someone important." She mumbled to the chilly breeze, as she contemplated bolting, but her fright overpowered her flight. Still sitting on the ground, she waited in suspense.

When Officer Henry spotted Daisy, he parked and got out of the car. "Hello child. Are you okay?" The man was wearing a business suit under a black winter coat. He shouted as he waved his arms in her direction and walked closer.

"Why in heaven's name are you out here in the cold sitting under a tree in the middle of winter?" Daisy squinted her eyes and tossed a look over her shoulder to see if there was anyone else sitting under the tree.

He must be talking to me. Oh, butter my butt and call me a biscuit! If he tells my mother I am in big fat trouble.

She hesitated to stand up, but she did, and moved closer to the man. In the corner of her eye, she spotted the stone a few feet away.

"Did my mama send you to look for me?" She wondered if Grace told anyone where she had gone, and hoped she hadn't. *We made a pinky promise, after all.*

He answered with a question. "What are you doing out in these parts all by yourself?"

Daisy really didn't want to answer that question truthfully for fear of all the trouble she'd find herself in, so she skirted around it temporarily with small talk. "Sir, that sure is a fancy car you're driving. Are you one of those European investors from the River Resort?"

He bit down on his lower lip, leaned in and gave her the stare. That stern look adults are so famous for when you're not answering their question. *Think quick!* She told herself.

Daisy came up with a satisfactory answer, the partial truth of why she was there. She put on her most serious face and informed the man. "It was a much warmer day when I left my house early this morning. The sun was shining beautifully in a clear summer sky. My friend was with me too, but she went back home and then I wandered out here on my bicycle and I got lost. I must have fallen and hit my head."

Not seeing her bicycle anywhere, and humored at the girl's imaginative version of the morning's warm weather the truant officer asked, "well kiddo, since your bicycle doesn't seem to be around here as far as I can see, how 'bout I give you a ride home and get you out of this cold?"

Her eyes darted back and forth from the stone on the ground to the man standing in front of her.

"My name is Officer Clark, and you are?" He asked sternly. "Wilhelm. Uh, WILLIAMS. Rose Williams," she lied. He extended his hand. "Pleased to meet you, Rose Williams." She extended her hand in return and they shook. "Thought I heard you say Wilhelm," he said. "I knew of a family by that name when I was growing up by the river. Their kid disappeared and the entire town looked for her all summer. It was a real heartbreak for the family.

She wasn't the first child to go missing, either. I don't know whatever became of the lost kids because my parents didn't want to live in a town where disappearances occurred, so we moved away before the end of that year.

And then, after the war in 1942, this town really started booming. That's when I was hired permanently to work within the education system as a truant officer, after a two year apprenticeship. I don't know why I'm telling you this." He couldn't help but notice the old camera she had hanging around her neck. "Anyway, sorry I'm rambling. Let's get you home now, Rose Williams."

Daisy wanted to make a run for it, but she was taught to respect her elders, so she did as she was told and followed him, but not before picking up the stone and hiding it in her camera bag.

The gravel crunched under their feet until they reached the paved road. Daisy jumped up into the 1950 Buick, happy to get out of the cold, and scanned around the interior. "Fascinating! Look at this shiny steering wheel and all those knobs on the dashboard. Where did you ever get an automobile like this one?" Henry laughed to himself.

With the distraction of discovering a 'modern' vehicle, it took her a minute before she got around to processing the story he told about the missing kids and something about 1942. She sat and thought about it for a while.

Could he be talking about the Harris brothers? And that Walter boy? And WHAT Wilhelm kid was he referring to?

She scratched her forehead with dirty fingers and stared out the window, looking at nothing. Her heart pounded like a drum inside her chest and she wondered if Henry could hear it, too. She also wondered about other things, but mainly how she came to be in this predicament. *Oh no! Is it possible I've time traveled again?*

Officer Clark punched the accelerator, pulled out of the field and drove several miles until he reached Riverside Drive.

"You a photographer?" He asked out of curiosity, pointing to the Kodak Brownie Box camera around her neck. Her mood lifted and her posture shifted. "Yes, sir. My daddy has a portrait studio at home, and he's teaching me all there is to know. He says I have a creative eye for a 14-year-old."

"Well, that's a good old-fashioned camera you have there, so be careful with it. They sure don't make 'em like that anymore." Affirmed Henry.

Yeah, no kidding.

They drove through a very different-looking town than Daisy recalled from earlier that morning when she was riding her bicycle with her best friend Grace. More houses and bigger trees. She recognized the road they were on because she saw the street signs and her school.

"You sure you live at the River Camp? I was under the impression that community hasn't been occupied since the war, except for some vacationers in the summer."

They passed her friend Grace's house and then he turned at the fork in the road. "See that big house on the hill? That's where one of this town's richest family lives. Huxley Dalton was one of the River Camp developers."

Daisy squinted her forehead. *Was?*

"Now his daughter lives there with her husband and their children. I only know that from reading the society page in our newspaper. Never met them."

Daughter? Grace? Daisy wondered.

The cigarette lighter on the dash popped. He rolled down the window and then lit a Marlboro.

Deep in thought, Daisy scrunched her forehead and looked back at the house in the distance.

"You are awfully quiet back there." Henry was making small talk. Daisy was busy contemplating what in the heck he was babbling on about and wished he'd stop talking such ridiculous nonsense.

"There!" She pointed at the cottages along the river. "My house is the 3rd one from the corner." Relieved, she was finally close to home. Henry pulled the car up to the curb and turned the engine off. He got out of the car and then opened Daisy's door. "Are you sure this is where you live?" They walked the path that led to her house, but Daisy approached cautiously.

This looks like the same house but it's distinctly different than it had been when I left earlier today. There were much smaller trees in the yard and I know that fence wasn't there. What year was this? Daisy was feeling nauseous, and she cried. She could taste the salty tears on her lips.

Slowly, Daisy opened the screen door and then turned the knob on the main entry door. It opened to an empty room. The green velvet sofa, her father's worn out chair where he read the newspaper every morning, her mother's rocker next to the window, the side table with the candelabra lamp, the sewing cabinet, all gone. There were no floral drapes on the windows anymore. It was just an empty, dusty house. Even the kitchen in the back was empty of any furnishings.

Peering out the window to the river, she noticed overgrown gardens and weeds growing through the cracks in the stone pathway. Next to the lilac bush, she saw a vertical board in the ground with what appeared to be the word 'Finney' and the date 1920-1935, carved into it. She raced out the door to validate what her eyes saw. "No!" She yelled, and then she wept buckets.

Back inside, Daisy ran up the stairs to further investigate, only to find her little loft area stripped bare. Her bed, the clothes wardrobe, toys, her bookshelf, everything gone. She stormed down the stairs trembling with anxiety and missed the bottom step. She landed hard and hit her head.

"Rose," he slapped her face gently. "Can you open your eyes? Rose!" When she didn't respond, Officer Henry scooped her up off the floor, grabbed the fallen camera and quickly carried her to his car.

Fourteen

THE ORPHANAGE

Two days after Henry rushed her to the trauma hospital, he received a phone call at home. "Rose opened her eyes this morning," informed the doctor, "and she pulled through like a champ, except she doesn't seem to remember who she is."

A nurse was sitting beside the child's bed, caressing her slender hand. Daisy stared ahead like she was in a trance.

"Perhaps you can come in today and visit with her, and help her recall the incident? That may jog her memory." Henry replied, "I'm on my way. Thank you, doctor."

"My name is not Rose. What happened to me?" She was trembling and had tears streaming down her face. "Are my parents here?" "Rose," explained the doctor, "we're looking for your family right now. Can you tell me where your parents live?"

Henry arrived and rushed into the room just in time to answer the doc's question. While he was recounting the story in detail, Daisy took one look at him and everything rushed back into her memory. More horrifying than being carried away by a flash flood. The empty cottage, the overgrown shrubs in the yard, the fancy car she rode in, the lie she told about her name.

Afraid to say a word, she made the decision not to speak for the time being. She remained mum except for the occasional 'ow' when she lifted her bandaged head.

With her identity a mystery, and not a single person phoning in looking for a missing child, the hospital director called the local newspaper. A few hours later, a reporter and photographer arrived. A photo captured Daisy sitting silently in her hospital bed, overcome with hopelessness.

"Once the story runs, we should have more information on her identity. Someone has to be missing their child." The doctor informed Henry, out of Daisy's earshot. "I'll stop in tomorrow after the morning edition gets delivered." Henry said. "For now, we wait and hope." Then he said goodbye to the doctor, the nurse, and 'Rose.'

The Daily Sentinel printed a full-page story of the little lost girl found by a stranger. Her photo shown front and center above the article that read:

DO YOU KNOW ROSE?

On Tuesday afternoon, truant officer, Henry Clarke, rushed a young girl to Hackensack Hospital. He found the girl, cold and alone, at Oakland Park when he was driving in the area. She told him she went for a bicycle ride earlier that day and got lost. The whereabouts of her bike is unknown, as it was not with her at the scene.

The officer offered to drive her home and when they

got to the house she had claimed to live in; they found it completely empty and abandoned. Distraught, the girl tumbled down the stairs and hit her head.

Rose is 14 years old, 5 feet tall, and has two different colored eyes. Rose is confused about her identity and her address. If you recognize her, please call your local police station or the hospital.

Grace was sitting down for a quick breakfast before work, when the paperboy knocked on the door. He handed her the morning's edition and collected the weekly payment. Normally, she read the paper in the evening, but today she had a little extra time. The fresh ink was pungent. She unrolled the paper and scanned the front-page headline.

"Her family must be devastated." Grace thought after reading the article. "I can't imagine the anguish they must feel. I'm sure when today's paper circulates, someone will surely recognize the child."

Grace scribbled a note to her boys: Do you know who this girl is? Perhaps a classmate? And clipped it to the page.

She glanced at the paper again. "How unusual to be born with two different eye colors." She was reminded of her best friend Daisy, and recalled the year when she disappeared. Tears welled in her eyes. She opened her purse and pulled a photo from her wallet. Two best friends posing together. Daisy wearing her polka dot chiffon dress.

⌒℮◠

Grace married young. After Daisy disappeared the summer of '24, she leaned on her only other friend, Al. And five & a half years later, at age 20, they tied the knot.

A highly sought after seamstress, Grace managed to squeeze in upholstery jobs several times a week. She was a devoted wife and mother, so her outside work came second.

Most of her clients were in the wealthier part of the city and meeting with them required a 20 minute commute via the Erie Rail. On this morning, the weather was beautiful, so Grace opted for a walk instead of driving to the train station.

As she strolled along Union Avenue, she thought about the Sentinel's headlines. Normally she'd listen for the birds chirping and admire all the glorious nature along her route, but not today. She felt dispirited thinking of the poor little girl with no identity, and overwhelmed by how oddly familiar her face looked.

⌒℮◠

It didn't take Daisy long to figure out she time hopped FIFTY YEARS to 1949. *Why'd I have to be so curious? I had no intention of traveling again. I just wanted to find out what the sacred site and time travel had in common.*

Officer Clark checked in with Daisy every week at St Mary's orphanage. No one had stepped up to identify her since the news story broke and bringing her there was the only option.

Week after week, he always got the same report from

the sisters. "She's polite when spoken to, but otherwise keeps to herself and doesn't say much. Sometimes we forget she's even here. She spends a little time in the sewing room helping the smaller children cut their squares for the quilt. And every so often we'll find her in the garden muttering to herself about yellow tornadoes and rocks. I think she's outside reading right now. She's always got her nose in a book, that one.

I'll go fetch her." Sister Maria could talk for hours. Time Henry didn't have. "Don't bother, sister. I'll go out to the garden. I have something I'm sure she'll be very excited about."

Daisy knew that keeping quiet and to herself prevented her from slipping up and talking about her mysterious circumstance. She didn't think they'd believe her and feared they'd think she was nuts after hearing it. She didn't mind spending time with the children because they didn't ask questions.

But Walter Moore was another story.

Walter snuck up behind her one morning while she was sitting outside in the garden reading. "Time travel, huh? How informed are you about that?"

Daisy slammed the book shut and turned it over.

"Forgive my intrusion. I'm Walter, resident groundskeeper." He held out his hand, but she didn't reciprocate. Walter's intrusion into her private space agitated Daisy. She crossed her arms and tightened her lips. And then, thankfully, Henry showed up, and she hoped Walter would get lost.

"Hey Rose!" Henry called out as he walked down a winding path trimmed with pretty spring tulips of all colors. "You'll never guess what I found in the trunk of my car." "What?" Asked Daisy.

He held up her Brownie Box Camera. Daisy, overwhelmed with emotion, sprang from her chair. She grabbed it out of his hands and hugged him. First gladness, then sadness, and the latter showed on her face. "Oh Rose, I thought this would make you happy." "Thank you. It should indeed. And I'm grateful to have it back."

Daisy opened the case and looked inside. She lifted the camera just a teeny bit with her fingers and felt around for the diary. *It's still here. Whew!* She gazed up at him with the saddest eyes. "Henry, I have photos on this camera of the people who are no longer here with me, and the thought of that makes me wretched sad." She turned away and sat back down. She slumped in the chair.

"Hold on. You say you have photos in that box?" "Why, yes, I do. I've several on this roll of film." A moment of realization came to them both at the same time and they spoke at once. "Let's develop the film!"

Daisy thought to herself. *These photos can support my story if I ever get the nerve to tell Officer Henry the truth.*

Henry was thinking. *These photos may help us discover her identity."*

Neither noticed that Walter was standing off to the side, watering the flowers, and listening with elephant ears. "I have to find out more about this girl and her peculiar interests in time travel."

"Indeed, this is wonderful progress." Sister Maria slapped both her aged hands together in a prayer pose and grinned from ear to ear. Henry didn't realize she had followed him outside.

The skirt of the sister's habit dragged ever so lightly on the ground as she hurried across the garden to share their epiphany with the other nuns. Something Henry and Rose would have preferred she kept to herself.

February 16, 1950

Dear Diary - I'VE MISSED YOU! I'm in an orphanage, of all places. They think my name is Rose and they're attempting to figure out who my family is.
It's all very confusing.

I've been here for months and as soon as I FIGURE OUT HOW to get back to 1924, I'm leaving!

I got my camera back. I feared I had lost it forever. Fortunately, this diary was still in the case, tucked away on the bottom.
Whew!

PS. Walter is a pain in the rear. There's something peculiar about him and I WISH he would QUIT snooping on me.
He has nothing better to do?
I'll write more later.

Daisy

February 19, 1950

Dear Diary - Officer Henry removed the film
from my camera. He's taking it to get
photo prints made.
He thinks the photos will help him figure
out who my family is.

BOY IS HE IN FOR A SURPRISE! He should
be back with the photos any day now.
I'll write soon.

Daisy

MOMENT OF TRUTH

Five days later, Henry returned to the orphanage to
share the four 2-1/2 x 2-1/2 inch prints from the developed film roll, with Daisy.

It was early when he arrived and she and her room-
mates were barely awake. Footsteps approaching from
the hall were heard, followed by an anxious knock on the
door. "Who is it?" "Rose, it's Officer Henry. Please get
dressed and meet me downstairs in the library."

He handed her the photos. One by one, she studied
each of them, teary-eyed.

The first one of Grace. She was sitting on the bank
of the river, leaning forward ever so slightly, her knees

tucked up under her long gingham skirt. Daydreaming and twirling a flower in her hands, listening to nature sounds.

"I wonder what she's doing now. My very best friend in the entire world." Her voice trailed off into a cloud of sadness. "Her name is Grace Dalton. She lives in the house up on the hill we passed the day you discovered me in the park." Henry made a mental note to check on the Dalton family.

The second photo showed Katherine and Charles standing in front of their cottage, both wearing formal attire from that time period. "These are my parents." Daisy turned the photo around for Henry to see.

The third photo is of Daisy and her mother, Katherine. Daisy, a year younger than she is now, dressed in that same old-fashioned clothing. "And this is my mother and I." With her arm stretched all the way out, she held the photo close to Henry's face.

Daisy looked at each photo one more time with tears streaming down her face, and then handed them back to Henry.

He pointed at the young girl in the photo and asked, "Rose, you say this girl in the photo here, is you? Standing next to your mother?" He half chuckles. Unconvinced, he says, "How can that be? This photo looks to be rather old. As a matter of fact, just look at the style of their clothing. Nobody dresses like that anymore. Are you sure this young girl isn't actually your mother and the older woman your grandmother? I do see a resemblance between you, but I have my doubts this is you pictured.

Daisy realized what she was saying made no sense to him because he had no idea of the truth. She thought it was time to share her bizarre story with him. She contemplated while he continued flipping through the photos.

"And this one, of the girl you call Grace. Where is she now?" "I don't know," she replied sharply. "She's my best friend and I miss her terribly. If she were here, she'd know what to do."

"Officer Henry, if I confide in you, can I trust that you'll believe me? And not think I'm crazy and send me off to some godforsaken place to be locked up?" His forehead wrinkled as he looked on in question. "What precisely are you trying to tell me?" He leaned in closer.

A minute later there was a knock on the door and Sister Maria came in with two books. Henry straightened up in his chair.

"Here they are, Rose, the books you were waiting for." "Thank you, sister." Daisy stood up and stuck out her hands to retrieve the books.

"It sure is an unusual subject for a young girl to be researching. I'll return them for you when you're finished, dear. You have 10 days before they're due back to the library." Sister Maria left the way she came in, minus the books.

Daisy placed the books on the sofa and sat down next to them. The delivery was perfect timing, in her opinion. Henry peered in their direction, a questionable look on his face.

'The Science Behind Time Travel'
'Thermodynamics'
'Native American Rituals'

Really? You're reading these? Whatever for?"

Rose replied harshly. "Whatever for? Haven't you been listening to a word I've told you?" She inhaled slowly. "I'm sorry for snapping." Officer Henry looked confused. She went on to say, "I've been showing you photos of me that were taken in 1924, and here I am in 1949 and I haven't aged one bit. Geesh." Daisy smacked her forehead and glared up at Henry. "Why don't you believe me?"

"I want to believe you, but I've never met a time traveler before, and I have a lot of thoughts swirling around in my head." Henry was as perplexed by this situation as anyone else would be.

Daisy felt defeated. She pressed her hand on her chest to slow the heart palpitations and looked up at him with misty eyes. "I was born on May 8th, 1963. I'm not lying or crazy! I have no idea how I ended up here sitting with you, crying about my other life.

Can't you see? This is why no one has stepped up to claim their missing 14-year-old. It was 1924 when I went missing!" She questioned loudly, "Can you please trust I'm telling the truth?"

Henry leaned in, his eyes squinted. He was trying to follow her story without passing any judgment. Daisy was agitated. There was a constant tap on the floor with her foot as she told the details of her accidental time traveling.

"Before now, I was living with my family in the cottages on Riverside Drive. The same cottages we visited the day you found me. That being said, I only lived there a short time." Henry listened.

"In 1972, a man kidnapped me from Jungle Habitat. An animal sanctuary my 6th grade class was visiting." Deep lines appeared in Henry's forehead. "The man carried me to Live Oak Park, near the sacred burial site. I kicked and screamed the whole time, but he kept running.

It was in that park where I experienced a mysterious force that sent me back in time fifty years. I can't explain it. And then I met Charles. The year was 1922." "Charles?" Asked Henry. "Yes. He's the man who I call father now. He and his wife, Katherine, adopted me."

"If you check the newspaper archives from April 1922, you will find the article about the lost girl. I'm not making this up." "Rose," said Henry, "I don't think you're crazy, but I do suspect you have an active imagination."

He pulled out his handkerchief and waved it at Daisy to wipe her tears. "Nobody uses handkerchiefs anymore!" She tossed it to the side. "I'd rather use a tissue."

Daisy stood up and walked over to the window. Snowflakes were falling from the sky. "There won't be much snow today," she observed. "How do you know that?" "Big snow little fall, little snow big fall." "Huh?" Henry had never heard the phrase before. Daisy ignored him and sat back down.

"Okay, I have an idea." Henry changed the subject. "Tell me something about the future. What's it like?"

Daisy tilted her head and chewed on her bottom lip. "The park where you found me, Live Oak Park, is called Memorial Park. That's what I've always known it to be called. There's a football stadium, and baseball and softball fields. I played softball there. I'm not sure when the name changed."

"Hmm." Henry seemed doubtful. "Softball for ten-year-old girls? You don't say." He had a look of uncertainty in his eyes and let out a sarcastic chuckle. Daisy gave him a dirty look. She was losing her patience.

"Okay. American Presidents. I learned all of them in Mrs. Bartlett's class; After Truman, there's president Eisenhower, then Kennedy, Johnson, and Nixon."

Henry questioned, "Kennedy? The war hero from Massachusetts?" Daisy shrugged. "I guess." Henry squirmed in his seat, crossed his leg, and adjusted his posture. "Well then, go on. You've got my attention."

"Oh! And, a man walked on the moon! Two, actually." Her eyes got really big. "Neil Armstrong and Buzz someone, in 1969. It was televised. My whole class watched it." Henry took a pen out of his pocket, opened his notebook, and scribbled the name Neil Armstrong. He glanced at Rose with skeptical eyes.

Searching for more fun facts, she looked up to the sky and thought a minute. "Okay. Look at this mark on my arm. It's from the smallpox vaccination I received when I was five or six. We all got one." "A smallpox vaccination? Men walking on the Moon? I do declare this is fascinating if it's true." Suggested Henry. "And how would someone my age have this knowledge if it were not true?" Daisy got defensive.

Henry stood up, hands in his pant pockets, and paced the library floor. "Let's start from the beginning. In 1963. What can you remember from your early childhood?"

Daisy thought about the question for a moment and then recounted what she could.

"I lived in a rundown old house. It was a two-story gray structure. Someone else lived downstairs. The front lawn was covered in ivy, and there were steps going up to the front porch. When I was a baby, my crib was in my mother and father's room. After he left, it was just my mother's room. I have vague memories of the room and both of my parents being together."

Henry listened intently, and she continued. "After I was older, I had my own room upstairs in the attic. It was called a finished attic. Not the scary kind. I got in trouble a lot because I didn't keep it clean."

"One year I was supposed to have a party for my ninth birthday. I was upstairs jumping around in my room and Charla yelled up the stairs. What are you doing? You're supposed to be cleaning! When I heard her coming up, I stashed everything under my bed. Well, she didn't fall for that trick because I had done it before. She pulled all the things out from under and piled it on top of the bed. Then, told me not to leave my room until I cleared the pile.

Later that day, she called off my party and made me go all around the neighborhood to inform everyone that we had canceled it. How embarrassing. She was a horrible person."

Henry formed his own opinion. "Well, that doesn't make her horrible. Heartless maybe."

Thinking of her past life saddened Daisy, but she continued, "My mother had parties all the time. The adults drank and got silly. I'd sneak out of the house and sit on the front porch steps, just to escape the noise.

One time, my mother's boyfriend found me outside and slapped me so hard my legs and back were covered in welts."

It was difficult for Daisy to re-live the experience. Her palms were sweaty, and she was fidgeting, but she continued. "In the mornings after a party, my mother would sleep late. I would get myself ready for school. I always looked like the kid who threw herself together in two minutes. My mother was never around during the day, and my father left us when I was little. Charla let me do what I wanted most of the time."

Henry rethought his last opinion as he shook his head in disbelief. "Yes, now she seems like a horrible mother."

Daisy wasn't finished. "On Fridays it was payday, and she'd go to the liquor store for whiskey and beer.

Whenever she got beer, I knew the boyfriend would be coming over. On Saturday afternoons, when my mother finally got out of bed, we'd go to the grocery store. I'd put away the groceries while my mother smoked a cigarette and sipped on her whiskey."

Daisy broke down in tears. Henry reached into his jacket and pulled out a handkerchief, then handed it to her. "I don't have a tissue." She wiped her eyes and nose and handed it back to him.

"So when I ended up in 1922 with the Wilhelms," her eyes widened as she knew she just slipped up on the name, but hoped he hadn't caught on, "I knew what a proper family was like. And I never planned to leave them."

Henry made a mental note of the last name he just heard. "So, you think you're a time traveler?"

$$\infty$$

The two sat quietly for a long while. The television from the room next door was blaring. Sister Maria loved to watch the 5 o'clock news. Officer Henry glanced at his watch. "Rose, do you still have the clothes and the shoes you were wearing the day I found you?" "Yes, I believe so. Shall I go get them?" "I'd like to have them authenticated if you don't mind. If you traveled here from 1924, they could be the missing link to back up your story." "Oh, that would be a wonderful relief! Then you believe me?".

"It's highly improbable, but I want to believe you." "Oh, thank you!"

Daisy leaped out of her seat and pulled Henry in for a big hug.

"What is this?" He asked, showing her the photo of the shrine.

February 27, 1950

Dear Diary, - Henry brought the photos today. Sadness hit me harder than I expected. WHY did I ever go BACK TO THAT WALL? Aaaaargh!!!
I don't think he believes my story even after seeing the old photos.

I'm so frustrated I cannot write another word!

Daisy

FIFTEEN

WALTER

The following afternoon, Walter cornered Daisy in the hallway. "WHAT?" "Easy there, tiger. Don't be so annoyed with me. I only want to ask you a few simple questions." "What kind of questions?" She asked. Walter motioned for her to follow him outside to the garden bench.

"I believe that there may be some similarities in our lives." "Oh?" She perked up. "And what would those similarities be?"

"Well, for starters," he cleared his throat, "we both ended up here from another time. And – I think there are others." Daisy was wide-eyed and didn't hold back her reaction. "How could you know that? I haven't said anything." She crossed her arms. "And what do you mean we both, and others?"

"I'll tell you what I mean. The 'others' are my friends; Tommy and Frankie Harris. When we were younger, we were always out going around getting into some kind of mischief," he laughed. One time we built a tree house in the woods and when we got bored with it we lit it on fire. We'd go around to the yards where we knew there were dogs, and we'd antagonize them so they'd run after us." "What does this have to do with me?" He really got under her skin.

"I'm gettin' there. We were on our bikes, so we always got away. One day, old Mrs. Miller came out with a big shovel in her hand, threatening to hit us. We were bad kids." He shook his head and then he laughed again.

As Daisy listened she had a startling thought. *Those MUST BE the boys I heard about. The ones who disappeared and never returned. Holy smokes!*

"We liked to play harmless tricks on other kids. One time we were out riding our bikes around town and Tommy called some boys over to come with us. He thought he was being funny. Hey, follow us, he yelled. And they did. Well, Tommy took a turn onto a dirt path leading to the woods. He stopped, and we all stopped. Then he yelled to the boys in the back, hey, we need to turn around and go the other way. So the boys took off, but we never followed. Instead, we raced through the trees until we lost them."

Daisy spoke up. "You know, Walter, those boys must have been the ones who told the police where you were headed. The whole town looked for you, for weeks. Eventually they figured you must have gone to the sacred site, because some kind of evidence was found there. Your disappearance is still one of the town's biggest mysteries. And you're also the reason that area is off limits now. Families won't picnic anymore, and children are forbidden to play near there."

"Let me finish the story." Afraid he'd lose his train of thought. "The three of us went to that big wall by the sacred site. Just as you mentioned. We were only looking for something to do that day. We saw the rocks and started tossing them around."

Daisy chastised him. "You didn't know that area was a sacred burial ground?"

"The idea that we could be disrespecting a sacred space never crossed our minds. We were acting like little assholes, but we didn't care."

Daisy was drawn into his story, listening intently.

"The last thing I remember is seeing Tommy in the center of a yellow tornado, and then he was gone. He disappeared into thin air. Then the same thing must have happened to me because the next thing ya know I wake up in a park by a big tree and it's 1939. I never saw Tommy or Frankie again."

"Holy Crap!" Daisy considered the possibility to be unimaginable. "The same strange force that brought me here brought you here too? This can't be a coincidence." "I think fate brought us together," he added his two cents. "But why?" She twirled a strand of hair around her finger. "That's what we have to figure out."

"Rose, this whole scenario has troubled me for the last ten years. And next thing I know, you're here out of nowhere, just like me, and you're reading time travel books. Bloody hell. I knew I had to talk to you."

Daisy stood up and paced a few steps. She looked at him quizzically. "Are you a Native American descendant by any chance?" "Gee, I don't know. Why do you ask?"

"There's a tribe from our area who was known for having exceptional abilities. One of them being able to time travel. Although that wouldn't explain why I could travel."

"Unless you're Native American too?" Walter wondered. "Well, you make a good point. Do you think I could have inherited the traveler gene from my father's family?" She'd been curious about this. "I was never told what nationality he is." "Well, now that is something to chew on. Or perhaps our ancestry has nothing to do with it. Maybe we were chosen for our uncanny ability to recognize extraordinary events."

Walter grabbed the box of Winston's that he kept rolled up in the sleeve of his white t-shirt. Then, lit a cigarette and blew a big puff of smoke into the air before putting the box back in his sleeve. She watched curiously.

"I tell ya Rose. I don't wanna go back. I like this era; the music, the cars, television, phones. And I have a girl, too, who I could never leave. We're getting married one day." Puffs of smoke filled the garden air.

Daisy watched the white cloud disappear. She had never tried a cigarette before. "Want a drag?" She took the cigarette and put it to her lips, inhaled, and then let out a big cough. She handed the cigarette back to him. He continued, "I have no plans to leave, but I wish I could tell my aunt I'm okay. I've tried to find her, but no luck. She must have moved out of the area, or maybe something worse."

"Wait! Your aunt? What's her name?" He replied, "Gertie." Daisy got wide eyed and blurted out, "YES! I know who she is. She works for my best friend's family as their cook. Grace told me that Gertie's nephew disappeared ten years ago." His curiosity was aroused. "Do you think she still works for them?" "I have no idea." "That could explain why she doesn't have a phone listing in her name. If she lives with them, the listing would be in their name."

Daisy blurted out some information. "I can tell you where she lived in 1924. It's that big red house on the hill. Reef Rd." Walter drew his hand to his mouth. It was the first time Daisy knew him to be speechless.

"In the event your aunt isn't employed by the family anymore, it's possible they know where she is. And when I do return to 1924, I can certainly look for her and let her know you're safe. Was it 1940 when you got here?"

"Yes. Give or take." "Have you been living here all this time?" He nodded yes. "When I aged out of care, they offered me a job and a room here. They've shown me a lot of kindness.

"My photo is on the lost children board by Sister Lorraine's office. Have you seen it?" No! Show me."

Daisy hoped these old hallways would soon be a distant memory, but with no immediate plan of escape she'd have to stay brave and cope.

The cork board hung on the wall at eye level. A sign at the top read:

St. Mary's Orphanage - 137 Cedar Road
The Lost Children
Isaiah 49:20 – Give place to me that I may dwell.

The names of children, some with photos, were tacked onto the board, along with the date they came to the orphanage and their age.

Jacob - 1912 - age 13
Katy - 1921 - age 8
Mari - 1930 - age 3
Walter - 1940 - age 16
Rose - 1949 - age 14

"Oh! So this is why they took my photo when I arrived?" Daisy ran her finger up and down, along the dates. "Well this is uncanny." "What is?" Walter looked uncertain. "Each child arrived nine years apart. Except you. – I know you don't believe in coincidences, Walter, but how else would you explain this?"

"I did arrive in 1939, but I wandered the streets for a short period of time before Officer Henry brought me here." "Aaaah." Daisy tapped her chin."

I need a picture of this. Stay here." She dashed down

the hall to go get her camera.

February 28, 1950

Dear Diary - Walter isn't the creepy lurker
I believed him to be.

Get this - He only started following me
around once he noticed that I was reading
the time traveler books. He told me he
thought I arrived here THE SAME WAY HE
DID! Whaaaat? Boy, was I shocked to hear
him say that.

And guess what else? He is GERTIE'S
MISSING NEPHEW! Yep! How crazy is that?
This is so exciting my heart is pounding out
of my chest.

I wish I could share this wonderful news with
Grace! I miss her so much.

Daisy

Sixteen

A FORTUNATE DISCOVERY

Henry wanted to do some private investigating to verify what Daisy revealed about her past. Hoping to meet with her friend Grace, he drove to the estate where Daisy told him Grace lived. Henry remembered reading about the impressive house in high society magazines. The previous owner, Huxley Dalton, investor of the riverfront vacation town, died several years ago, from polio. He left behind his wife Elizabeth, daughter Grace, and son Thomas.

Henry wasn't sure who occupied the house now, but he'd never know unless he went there. After three knocks on the front door, a young man about 14 years old answered. "Good morning. Is Grace home by any chance?" Henry inquired. "I'm pretty sure she is out for a while, but I'll confirm with Gertie. Please, come in." Henry entered into the grand foyer and looked around. *Quite impressive.* He thought to himself.

A heavyset gray-haired woman who appeared to be in her 60s, dashed into the room and extended her hand. "Good afternoon sir, I'm Gertie. I run the kitchen here."

Henry shook her hand. "My name is Henry Clark. Would it be possible to speak with Grace for a moment? We aren't acquainted but I believe we have a mutual friend." "Oh. I'm so sorry Mr. Clark, but Grace isn't home at the moment." Henry was visibly disappointed and quick to leave. "Alright. Please ask her to call the number on this card anytime between 9am to 5pm. Good day."

"Out of curiosity Mr. Clark, who is the mutual friends?" "A young girl named Rose Williams." "Thank you. I'll let Grace know you were here. Good day then." Gertie watched him walk to his car before she closed the door.

⌒ℓᴐ

A few days later, Henry returned to the orphanage. Sister Maria greeted him in the foyer. "Hello Officer Clark. Are you here to visit Rose again?" "Good Morning sister, yes I am." He wore a broad grin. "I'll fetch her. She's at the breakfast table sitting with Walter, our gardener. They've been exchanging whispers for over an hour." She shuffled along the corridor while shrugging, as if she had no idea what those two may be talking about.

Daisy showed up a short while later, greeted Henry, and the two went outdoors to find a shady area in the garden on this unusually warm spring day. Henry spotted the white bistro table under a willow tree. "This is ideal. Let's sit." Daisy flicked a bug off the table before taking her seat.

"I come here often to read, as it's away from prying eyes, and reminds me of my yard at home." A quiver in her voice could be heard whenever she spoke about her home.

Henry rubbed his hands together and declared in a very serious tone, "I visited the Dalton's estate a few days ago." Her eyes bulged, and she leaned in closer. "Grace wasn't home, but I did meet the kitchen manager. Do you remember if they employed kitchen help in your time?" "Yes. A cook named Gertie. Of course I remember. She always gave us generous servings of ice cream after school." "I met Gertie." He informed her.

"You did? I'm so glad she's still with them." *I must tell Walter the news.* She thought to herself. Henry looked at her quizzically and then drew his hands together and rubbed his thumbs on his palms. He stared away for a moment, thinking. "You say you knew Gertie? Are you sure you haven't been snooping around that house recently? Maybe you're confused as to how you know her," he suggested.

"I'm NOT confused." Exasperated at the notion, he still did not believe her. Daisy stood up and flailed her arms. She faced him and shouted. "I've not been snooping around anywhere."

Henry motioned for her to sit back down. "Sorry. But, you do realize the subject of time travel is speculative?" He was someone who believed in proof through science. "No. It's not in my case. I have experienced it, therefore it's the truth."

"Let's start at the beginning," he suggested. Daisy's face lit up, excited to spill, finally. "Tell me everything."

"The plan was a secret I dreamed up several years after moving in with the" ... she hesitated before blurting out her real name, again. "My new family. My curiosity about time travel and my experience was one thing. However, after I learned about the boys who disappeared, I was fascinated about the idea that others also traveled." She shifted in her seat and tapped her fingers on the table. "Rumor had it that someone saw them heading in the direction of some sacred Indian site, or sacred wall, as some would call it, right before they went missing."

"Yes, I remember hearing about that, too." Henry told her. "They weren't the first kids to disappear, either. Soon after that happened, we moved to another town."

Daisy continued her story. "I pestered my mother to tell me more about the disappearance, but she had no additional details and told me to stop asking questions. Grace reminded me that Native Americans lived in Waterloo, the next town over, long before we settled in. I visited Waterloo on a class trip in 1970 and remember learning something about rituals for the dead that took place in a sacred area by a big wall."

She slapped her hand down on the table and, with a very determined look, continued. "Well, that didn't stop my curiosity, so I started researching at the library and that's when I discovered it was the same place my abductor brought me to in 1972."

"A brilliant idea, Rose. You're a smart cookie." Henry praised her. She rolled her eyes and picked up where she left off.

"I made a plan to go find the wall the day our summer vacation started. I included Grace on the plan because I didn't want to go alone, but I didn't tell her the real reason for the excursion. She thought I wanted to take a photo for entry into a contest." Daisy continued for 30 minutes reliving that morning in perfect detail until Henry got the whole picture.

"Daisy, I hope you understand how preposterous this sounds." She nodded, yes. Henry continued. "Well, I've yet to get any lab reports back from your clothing, but I'd like to go visit the area you're talking about." "Today?" "Yes," he answered. "I'm coming with you! But first, there's something I need to do. I'll be right back." She ran off before Henry could stop her.

"Walter, Walter!" Daisy saw him watering plants in the garden and sprinted his way. Alarmed, he tossed the hose aside and raced her way. She stopped to catch her breath before blurting out. "Your aunt. She still lives with the Dalton family." The hose squiggled wildly and water squirted in different directions. "Walter, turn the hose off. I'm getting soaked." Daisy insisted. And they both laughed.

"Okay, okay, tell me how you know this?" "Officer Henry went there to look for my friend Grace and her son answered the door but didn't know the whereabouts of his mother so he asked the kitchen manager." "Rose, slow down." "Okay, sorry." She took a breath and continued. "The woman came out and introduced herself to Henry as Gertie. Walter! You can go see your aunt and tell her you're alive!"

Walter looked like the most grateful human being on the face of the earth right now. "Unbelievable! I owe this miracle reunion all to you, Rose. I've been looking for her for 10 years. You've been here for six months and solved the mystery."

"No, this was truly by chance, no solving was implemented." He replied, "I don't believe in chances. Our crossing paths was meant to be. You understand that, right?" "I suppose I'm beginning to now."

Daisy tilted her head to the side and peered at the ground. "Walter, I have a confession to make." He seemed so genuine, and she was overcome with guilt for lying to him. "Can I trust you not to tell the others?" He creased his brow. "Yes you can trust me, of course."

Daisy went on to explain that her name really wasn't Rose and that she only lied because she didn't want her parents to find out she had ventured to the forbidden grounds on that day she disappeared.

"When Henry found me, I was afraid he'd bring me home and tell my parents where I had been. So I made up a name. I didn't learn until later that I traveled to a different year, and it felt awkward telling him the truth at that point, so I let him go on calling me Rose."

Walter gave her a hug. "Don't worry, kid. I won't tell anyone. And thank you for trusting me. Now, how do I explain to my aunt why I'm 20 years younger than I should be?" She shrugged her shoulders. "You'll figure it out.

Now go see your aunt. And bring me back a full report about Grace. Please don't tell her I'm here. I want to go back to 1924 and grow up with her as if none of this has ever happened. I miss my best friend so much."

"Oh! One more thing. I told Officer Henry all about the sacred site and he wants to see it. But don't worry, I didn't mention you." Walter unrolled his shirt sleeve and pulled out a Marlboro. "When are you going?" He flicked the lighter and lit the cigarette before taking a long inhale. Puffs of smoke filled the air a few seconds later. "We're going there today, and "I'll fill you in as soon as we get back." Daisy waved the cigarette smoke away with her hand.

"Now go! Go find your aunt."

Seventeen

ETCHINGS ON STONES

Grace had one more stop before heading home to her house on the hill. She turned into the parking lot of Carver's Luncheonette and parked at one of the two available spots close to the front door. She got out of her Cadillac convertible and retrieved three bolts of upholstery fabric from the back seat.

This was her last client of the day and she hoped the appointment would be quick. Her husband agreed to allow her to work as long as she finished by noon every day, and today she was cutting it close.

Working outside the home was practically unheard of for women in the 1950s, especially when the job was so demanding. But as long as Grace was home to prepare dinner for the family, Mr. Gibson approved without debate.

Henry and Daisy hurried inside to let Sister Maria know they'd be going out for a few hours. Daisy ran up to her room to grab a few items. "This may be my only chance to get back to 1924, but I won't be telling this to Henry."

She made a quick entry in her diary and then grabbed a sweater, her camera, and some personal items, including the $12 she had saved from Henry's weekly offerings. He'd often hand out dollar bills to the children when he visited, and Daisy saved most of hers.

"I don't know how to get to the park unless we start at the Paper Mill." Daisy informed Officer Henry. "Everything looks so different because so much has changed over time. The improved roads winding every which way, and the houses, so many big houses and shops. I'd hardly think this could be the same area." She continued pointing out all the changes. "It's amazing, really.

I wonder what Grace's thoughts are about the progress? She's 40 years old now. Oh, Henry, I wish you would have seen her the day you stopped by the house. I'm dying to hear everything about her life."

Henry, still questioning her story, threw this in for a test: "You seem surprised at the changes here, but I imagine this town had substantial growth by the 70s. The town must be a different scene in the future." "I guess." Daisy had no recollection of this particular area. "I lived on the other side of town, closer to the train station.

We didn't always have a car, and almost never ventured past our neighborhood. Charla and I walked to wherever we needed to go. Even Dairy Queen was nearby, but that was only open in the summer." "Dairy Queen?"

He questioned. She kept talking. "I recall a florist, an office supply store, and a pet store.

Seldom did I ever go down by the river, except for the season I played softball. The coach picked me up and drove me home. We'd talk game-play from the minute I got into the car, so I never paid attention to the sights we passed along the way.

See that bridge up ahead? That's where you turn. The paper mill is on the other side of the river." Henry followed his co-pilot's directions. "For 14 years old, she's quite the know-it-all," he came to notice. But impressed none the less.

When they pulled up in front of the mill, now a building twice the size as it once was, Henry pulled into the lot. "I remember a boat dock over there, and a bait and tackle shop." Her voice sounded eager. Daisy pointed to the far end of the building. "Where the boys wasted hours skimming rocks or doing who knows what that boys do."

A big smile formed on Henry's face as he recalled his youth. "I remember back in my day hanging down by that river."

Daisy continued with her narration. "Now in its place is a gas station, and next to that, Carver's luncheonette." "I can see that," he chuckled. She smirked at him.

"I'm thirsty Officer Henry. May I please have a fountain soda from the luncheonette? Please!" "Sure, why not. We have plenty of daylight time before the sun sets."

He shoved his car into reverse, made a u-turn and parked the car in front of Carver's, right next to a spiffy convertible.

Daisy pushed the restaurant door open, skipped to the counter, and hopped up onto a stool. Henry sat down next to her and gave his stool a spin. She laughed to see a grown man spinning on a counter stool.

They took no notice of Grace working at the far end, nor did she of them. "I'll have a chocolate soda pop, please." Daisy smiled at the waitress behind the counter. "Same for me," said Henry.

A short while later, Grace said goodbye to her client, the owner of Carver's. She picked up her fabric bolts, then walked toward the exit door. "On second thought, I'll have a soda."

She leaned the fabric against the counter and sat a few seats away from Daisy. The waitress came over. "Hi again Mrs. Gibson, what can I get you?" "I'll have what she's having." She pointed to Daisy. "It looks like a chocolate soda?" "You guessed it. Would you like whipped cream too?" "Sure, why not?" "How's Mr. Gibson?" "Oh, he's fine. Thank you."

Grace glanced a few times at the young girl slurping on her soda and spinning in her chair. Those long caramel braids reminded her of a friend long ago, which roused so many emotions she had kept tucked inside for 25 years. She parted her lips to take a sip of her fancy drink, and a tear dropped onto the whipped cream.

Grace finished her drink, paid the bill, grabbed the fabric bolts and headed to the exit. She glanced back to take one last look at the girl, and noticed Daisy's hair tie fell to the floor.

Grace paused, then turned to walk the few steps back to the counter to help retrieve the accessory. She met Daisy's eyes as she held out her hand, gesturing for her to take the ribbon. The two exchanged silent glances. "Thank you," replied Daisy.

Daisy took notice of a strand of blond peeking through the woman's dark hair and gasped. *Grace? Could it be?* Her heart skipped a beat. Daisy wanted so desperately to know if this woman could be her best friend, but she knew how crazy she'd appear if she mentioned anything, so she didn't.

Grace nodded and then turned to walk out the door. But she stopped. She thought hard and wondered what about the girl that seemed familiar? "Not the braids. It's more than that. If only I had more time, I could go back and talk to her." Just then, Henry called out, "let's go Rose."

Hearing the name Rose, Grace remembered the newspaper article last year about the unidentified girl. She assumed she was that Rose. "Ah, yes. That's why she seems familiar. She's the girl who was missing. I'm sure of it."

Daisy watched the older version of her best friend Grace, dressed in a two piece couture suit saunter out the door.

She's the most beautiful lady, wearing the fanciest clothes I've ever seen. I'm not positive that you're my Grace, but I like imagining that you are.

"Earth to Rose! Let's hit the road." Henry's impatience designed his tone. Before they exited, Daisy selected a postcard from the rack, handed the cashier $1.00, and waited for her change of 95 cents.

As soon as they were in the car, Daisy added the postcard to the collection of mementos from the future already stored in her camera box.

The postcard depicted a photo of Carver's Luncheonette on the front and the address printed on the back. To her excitement in tiny print, the words photograph by C.D. Wilhelm Photo Studio. The hair on her arms stood straight up into the air.

"Could C.D. be Charles? He must have his own photography business now. Where do they live though?"

For the next several minutes, Daisy remained in deep thought. Although she was unsure of the Wilhelms' current location, she reasoned that since Charles took the picture for the postcard, they must still be nearby.

The route to the site looked different from when Daisy and Grace ventured there in 1924. The old gravel road was miles long, and paved, which accommodated fast moving traffic.

People drove past the sacred site every day without even noticing anything might be hidden beyond the acres of oak trees and other forest growth.

"I've never been down this road," said Henry. "Could that be the wall you're looking for up ahead?" It was a clear day, and the structure was slightly visible, even though they were still some distance away. "Could be. Let's go find out." Daisy didn't hesitate to express her excitement.

Henry found a place to park and after they got out of the car Daisy led the way, nervous wobbly legs and all. She paused to scan the area and after a minute, continued walking. "Hard to imagine I was here less than a year ago, but in your world it's been 25." She struggled to grasp the implications of her predicament. "The great mystery of time travel."

Unhurried, they strolled through the open field, an uneven ground of dirt and weeds. Henry noticed Daisy seemed a little more upbeat than usual. "This entire experience is perplexing. Like a crazy dream. Isn't it Henry?" A tree branch swiped his head, so he brushed the obstacle aside with his arm.

"Yes, Rose, this entire story is more like an exaggerated hoax than anything. But we'll call it perplexing for now. I want to believe you." He shook his head, still not 100% convinced of her story.

When they approached the wall, Daisy couldn't contain her excitement. She went on and on with stories of both times in the past that she was here. First, in 1972. And she described the scene to Henry so he could picture it in his head. "This wall was almost completely covered in Ivy and weeds. And over here, do you see this hole? That's the hole I crawled into, which was much bigger at the time. I should clarify, it will be much bigger in the future." Henry crouched down for a closer look.

"My kidnapper put a chain around my ankle right in this very spot." She lifted her pants to show him the scar on her ankle. Henry's eyes showed some curiosity, and he admitted she started to sound more convincing.

She briefed Henry on all the development that will occur over the next 50 years. "In the future, this park will be completely surrounded by a new home community. A large section of the park will be preserved for an animal sanctuary. The one where my abduction took place.

How strange to know things that others don't." "You can say that again," replied Henry. "So, what else can you tell me about the 70s?" He leaned against a tree to rest.

She considered his inquiry, then peeped at his baseball cap sporting the Brooklyn Dodgers logo in front. "Well, the New York Mets won the world series in 1969. I was only six, but I remember the celebration and a parade." She conveniently recalled that dumb poster that hung in her living room. "The who? Never heard of 'em," he replied.

"And there is no Brooklyn Dodgers. They've been

called the Los Angeles Dodgers ever since the team moved to California." Daisy broke the news with no tact. Henry put his hand up. "Stop. I'm sorry I asked." He laughed and shook his head.

"Either she's pulling my leg or she's not, and knows way more about baseball than most girls." He reasoned.

Daisy continued. "And in 1924, this park looks much different. Newer. The sacred stones encircle the entire wall. It stayed like that for hundreds of years until the land development started."

Henry enjoyed their conversations. Rose, age 14, going on 19, in his opinion. She knew a little about a lot of things and certainly more than most kids her age. She was indeed a unique individual.

Henry watched as Rose wandered over to the wall and searched around as if she was looking for something. Moving the dirt around with her foot, digging it into the ground as she walked the perimeter of the wall.

I've got to figure out how to get back without Henry catching on. I don't know how he'd like my idea if I told him."

She knelt down and touched the wall, looking for loose bricks. "There are stones hidden in these walls. I need to find one." Henry rolled his eyes but kept watching. "Here! Look, I found a pretty one."

Rose held up a stone and then stood up. She turned the rock over to expose an insignia carved into the back. "This one has the "Friend" symbol on it. Two arrows." She told him to hold it.

"People of this tribe were given a particular gift. When they died, a stone was carved to represent their gift, or character, and then placed inside this wall as a sort of burial. As a matter of fact, two stones were carved. The second stone was placed at the bottom of the wall alongside other stones."

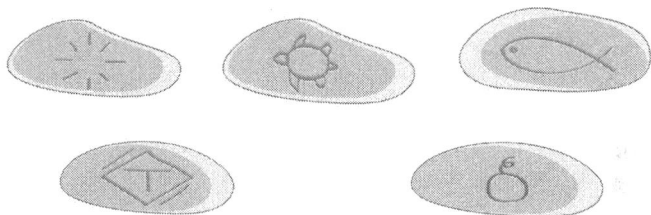

Henry was intrigued by her knowledge and wondered why he'd never heard this before.

"At one time, there were hundreds of stones here, but over the years they've gone missing. They should fence it in so people stay away."

"Do you think you should poke around here disturbing it, then?" He asked. Daisy felt like Henry was reprimanding her. "I'm not disturbing anything," she huffed. "I'm looking for a certain stone to show you." Partial lie.

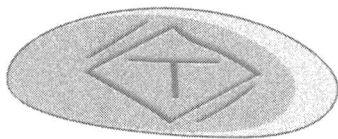

She stuck her arm into a small opening and felt around. "Here's another one!" Daisy spied the 'Travel'

insignia on the back. And it started to spark. She opened her palm and held it out for Henry to see.

The next thing happened so fast.

$$\sim\!e\!\circlearrowright$$

Henry watched in bewilderment as a cylinder shape of yellow translucent light formed from the ground then spiraled around her body. And just as quick as he lunged forward to grab her, she vanished.

He picked himself off the ground and wiped his hands against his pants to get the dirt off. Henry crashed to the ground, scraping his elbows and hurting his knees. He looked around in every direction, beyond puzzled. "What in heaven's name happened here?"

He spent the next 45 minutes looking through bushes and up in the trees. He doubted she'd play a trick on him, but if she did, this was cruel. He paced the area surrounding the sacred wall. Nothing looked out of place. "Well, gee whizz! Is it possible that she was really a time traveler after all?" Seemingly perplexed, he considered what to do next. "I've got to report this disappearance. What will I tell them? A girl picked up a rock and then vanished?"

EIGHTEEN

SPRING 1925

HOME AGAIN

Curled up on the ground close to the edge of the sacred wall, Daisy slept. Spring had officially arrived. The blossoms were just beginning to bloom, squirrels were running from tree to tree in search of nuts. It was a warmer than usual day for this time of year.

Daisy opened her eyes, pushed herself up to a sitting position, and unbuttoned her sweater. The wall looked different from when she was there with Henry just moments ago. "I think it worked! I'm back. At least I hope I'm back."

She hoisted herself up over the top of the wall and leaned in to peer over the edge. Looking down at the center, she saw the beautiful stones arranged in a spiral pattern exactly like they were in 1924. "Incredible!" She slid down the wall, and when her feet hit the ground, she twirled and danced and jumped in excitement.

Daisy opened her hand to reveal the stone she picked up right before the tornado swept her away. She ran her fingers over the etching on the back, stuck it into the camera case and headed home.

Daisy was dressed in the style of clothing young girls wore in the 1950s. A flowered blouse tucked into denim pants, and the Converse sneakers that Henry bought for each kid in the orphanage. She accidentally left her sweater by the wall, but it didn't matter on this warm day, anyway.

Fear fluttered in her gut and up through her chest as she approached the outskirts of town, wondering if she had returned to 1924 or worse, another decade. "How will my parents react to these unusual clothes I'm wearing, and to me being back?"

She pulled the Carver's postcard out of her camera case, scanned it and then stuck it back in. "If the luncheonette is there, which I hope it isn't, I'll go in and look at the date on a newspaper."

Silence hung in the air on her long walk along the path overgrown with weeds and moss. Her legs were wobbly with anxiety, so she kept a slower than usual pace. *Why do things always take longer when you're in a hurry?*

"At last!" She spoke out loud when she recognized the place where she and Grace parted ways. *Oh, how I miss my best friend. There's much to share about my experience, but it will have to be the perfect time.* "And I have the photos of Henry, and the sacred site in my camera that I can show her. She'll be so excited to hear about the future." Daisy spoke quietly to herself.

Not having seen any 1940s or 50s style cars on the road, Daisy took that as a positive omen, but still proceeded with uncertainty. She continued a little further until she recognized her surroundings. "The paper mill should be right around the corner." A whirlwind of questions swirled in her head as she recalled every detail of her travel journey.

A black and white patrol car pulled up alongside her just as she spotted the paper mill. She stopped and turned in that direction. The officer exited his vehicle and walked around to face Daisy. His hands were on his hips, near the club hanging from his belt, although he doubted he'd need to resort to violence today.

"Hello. What are you doing out wandering around the streets? Skipping school?" "No sir." Her voice quivered. She was overcome with a sense of dread, and wondered if he noticed she was frozen with fear.

"Are you from around here?" "Yes, I live on Riverside Drive." "Oh, is that right? What's your name?" He glanced past her at the missing girl poster nailed to a tree and did a double take. "Wait! Are you...?" She followed his eyes to the tree. "Yes, sir," she was not accustomed to being interrogated.

A loud knock on the Wilhelms' door startled Katherine, but before she could get to it she heard the screen door screech open and saw her daughter, who hadn't been seen in 10 months, standing there. Daisy looked perfectly fine except for the unusual clothes she was wearing.

Daisy ran to her mom. They embraced, and cried. Katherine hugged her so much tighter than she'd ever hugged a person, ever. She took her daughter's face in both her hands, brushed the strands of hair away from her eyes, and then stared in unbelievable joy.

"Where have you been all this time?"

"Oh Daisy, what's happened?"

"Are you okay?"

"Did someone take you?"

Daisy continued to sob. She hated to see her mother cry. "I didn't mean for any of this to happen," cried Daisy. "This is all my fault." "What's your fault?" "All I wanted to do was take some photos of the ancient burial site for entry into a contest." She placed the stone on a nearby table and then wiped her eyes.

"Daisy, please tell me where you've been all this time. And why would you deliberately go there when I told you not to?" Katherine pulled her daughter close to her chest and wrapped both arms around her. "I'm sorry for shouting. I've just missed you so much." Katherine said in a whisper, while she stroked her head. "You smell like apple blossoms." "It's the shampoo." Daisy replied. "A scented shampoo?" Katherine questioned in disbelief.

Daisy still had no idea what year it was, and she remembered seeing the grave marker for Finney in the yard.

Daisy pulled back from Katherine's smothering hug, and cried out, "where's Finney?" But Officer Cuish interrupted.

He'd been standing in their parlor, witnessing the reunion and not saying a word until now. "Why don't we all sit down and give Daisy a moment to come to terms with this situation? It may even take her a few days or weeks even before she wants to talk about it."

Being an observant officer, he noticed Daisy place the stone on the table. He narrowed his eyes and gave it a quick glance.

"Mom, where's Finney?"

Katherine was so caught up in her curiosities that she didn't hear Daisy ask about the dog.

"Daisy, did someone take you somewhere? Please! It's okay to tell us."

Daisy sat still. Her face expressionless. And Katherine continued with her questions.

"Officer, where did you find her?"

"She was walking along the street near the paper mill when I noticed her. I thought it was odd that she wasn't in school and thought she'd skipped, so I pulled over. I didn't recognize her at first. She told me her name and where she lived. I saw the poster on the tree and realized who she was. Other than that, you know as much as I do."

Daisy wasn't ready to confess anything more, so they all sat in a somber silence for what seemed like forever.

Officer Cuish stood up and said, "I'll leave you two to catch up and come back tomorrow." He glanced again at the stone, trying to make out the etching on it.

"Thank you for bringing her home Lee. Charles is out on an assignment, but if you see him, please fill him in. I know he'll be overjoyed to know Daisy has come back to us. Also, can you send word to Doc to come by as soon as he gets a chance? I'd like him to check her over. I'll try phoning him, but he may be out on a call."

"Yes, ma'am. Goodbye, now." "Thank you Lee." It was a small town, so being on a first name basis wasn't unusual.

Phone? What year is this? Daisy looked around for the telephone and any other modern improvements, and hoped too many years hadn't gone by.

She observed a new collection of photos hanging next to the ones hung some time ago, and got up to get a closer look. "Who's this baby?" She asked, pointing at the photo of Katherine holding a six-month-old. Katherine stood next to Daisy. She placed her hand on her back and whispered into her ear. "That's Marion." "Marion?" Asked Daisy. *Why does she look so familiar?* "Yes, Daisy. I'll tell you more about her a little later."

"Where's Finney?" She asked again, desperate.

"Sweetheart, Finney is upstairs, napping on your bed. Why don't you go say hello. She'll be ecstatic to see you!"

NINETEEN

A MUCH ANTICIPATED REUNION

∽❧∾

THE MORNING AFTER DAISY'S RETURN

Grace barely slept after the telephone conversation with Mrs. Wilhelm the night before. She jumped out of bed when the sun rose, ran out of her room and down the hallway to wake Elizabeth.

"Mother, are you up? When can we go visit Daisy?" Grace was getting antsy. "We'll leave after breakfast on our way to school. Go get dressed now."

"But mom! I'd rather spend the day visiting with Daisy than go to school." "I know honey, but Katherine may have other plans. She hasn't seen her daughter in almost a year." "Do you know if she's okay? Did Mrs. Wilhelm tell you anything at all?" "She's well and un-harmed is the report I got. We didn't speak long."

The short walk to the river seemed longer than usual. "Mother, I'm more excited than ever, and so anxious to see my best friend."

Elizabeth noticed an upbeat hop in Grace's step this morning. "I understand, dear. But, remember, we need to be sensitive to her circumstances. We're still unsure of what happened."

"I hadn't thought about that. I'm just over the moon excited that she's back, and I suppose a short visit is better than nothing," added Grace.

Feeling anxious at the anticipation of their reunion, Grace swayed back and forth, waiting for the door to swing open. "Good morning. Please come in." Katherine made a motion with her hand. "I'm so glad you're both here." The three moved into the living room and exchanged hugs.

"Where's Thomas?" "He's at home with Huxley. We wanted to give the girls some time alone together." Replied Elizabeth. "Daisy is looking forward to that. She hasn't talked about anything else besides wanting to see Grace."

When Daisy heard the voices, she hurried down the stairs and ran right into the arms of her best friend. The two embraced and cried. A moment that brought tears to everyone's eyes.

"Daisy, your disappearance gave me the scare of my life." Grace hugged her even tighter. "My heart is pounding." "Mine, too." Replied Daisy.

"We've all missed you." Elizabeth wrapped her arms around Daisy and squeezed her tight. "Likewise." Daisy replied. "Gertie sends her love." Elizabeth handed Daisy a bag of fresh hot sticky buns. *I must remember to get the photo of Walter to her.*

"Grace, let's go to my room, where we can talk in private and catch up on everything." Both girls raced up the stairs like old times.

"Elizabeth, would you like to join me in the kitchen for a cup of coffee and small talk? It's been a while since we've seen each other." "Sounds great. I'd love to." "I was so happy about Daisy's return I baked a pineapple upside down cake this morning. It's her favorite. Would you like a piece?" "I never turn down desert for breakfast." Elizabeth laughed.

"I'm so relieved that I'm back home, you have no idea. Grace, there's so much I need to tell you. I'm bursting at the seams." "Daisy, you needn't talk about anything if you're not ready." "Don't be silly. I'm telling you everything! You won't believe the stories I have to share with you."

Daisy pulled Grace to sit on her bed. She grabbed the camera from her bookshelf and placed it beside Grace before sitting next to her. "I have all types of momentos to show you." "Momentos? From where?"

"It's time to go now, Grace." Elizabeth called out as she walked up the stairs to the loft. "I know you girls have a lot of catching up to do but the school bell's about to ring."

"Mom, we just got here." Elizabeth motioned for her daughter to come. "But mother!" Elizabeth raised her left brow. "School. Now!" "Bye, Daisy. I'll come back soon." Daisy waited for Mrs. Dalton to leave before she whispered in Grace's ear. "I have the most bizarre stories to share with you. You must come back soon."

∽℮∾

For the next several days, Daisy got acclimated to being in her old surroundings. The doctor found no indication of any bodily harm to her, nor did he notice any psychological challenges, which was great news. But she refused to talk about her disappearance, and that concerned the Wilhelms.

TWENTY

OFFICER LEE CUISH

Lee Cuish, a Native American descendant, was raised by his white mother, Bridget, in a neighborhood with mostly Irish immigrants. He learned a great deal about their heritage, but knew little about his father, who disappeared when Lee was eight.

It wasn't until Lee's teenage years that he learned about the extraordinary traits of his father's people during a school trip to the Waterloo Forge Museum.

Lee was fascinated to learn about an ancient burial ritual, which included a ceremonial dance to send the dead peacefully on their way.

Two stones were dedicated to the soul which passed. One stone was buried inside a wall (a makeshift mausoleum) and the other placed on the ground close to the earth. A unique symbol that represented the person and their characteristics was inscribed on the stones.

A display chart hanging on the wall at the exhibit showed the different symbols used for the stones and their meanings.

When Daisy returned after her disappearance, she had a stone with her, and Lee noticed a similarity between her stone and the stones used for ancient burials. He wondered where and how she got it, and wanted to get a closer look to confirm his suspicion.

A few days after he brought her home, Lee had a brilliant idea. *I'll pretend I'm there to check on the kid, and try to get a feel for their schedules without raising any suspicion. Once I know their routine, I'll come back and let myself in when nobody's home.*

⁓

A few knocks on the door prompted Finney to charge full speed through the living room, followed by Daisy just a few paces behind her. While there, Lee had a chance to chat with Charles, who assured him everyone was fine. Especially Daisy, who was doing surprisingly well enough to return to school. "That's great news," crowed Lee. "So, will you be going back Monday?" "That's the plan," replied Daisy. "I'm anxious to see my friends and get back to learning." "That's our whizkid for ya." Katherine grinned from ear to ear.

Lee obtained the information he went there for. There'd be no reason to stay longer. "I'll be getting on my way now. If there's anything you need, just reach out. Enjoy what's left of your weekend." Lee tipped his hat and let himself out.

Lee planned to watch the house and learn the family's routine. Their comings and goings. Once he had that figured out, he'd be able to enter the vacant home through the back door without being seen.

The morning after his visit, he parked the patrol car several doors down from the Wilhelms'. He planned to take as many days as he needed, but when he saw Katherine and Daisy leave the house, and Charles right behind them, he thought, "Excellent timing. This may be easier that I thought. I'll get in and out before Katherine returns.

"Why couldn't we wait for Grace so we could all walk to school together?" Daisy asked. "Because I need to get to West End bakery before they sell out of dough. They only make a certain amount each day, and when it's gone, it's gone."

Daisy expressed her displeasure by sulking. "I wanted to walk with her and Thomas. I'm in high school now."

"It's too soon to leave you out of my sight. You'll have plenty of days to spend with Grace."

Lee made his way around the side of the house. No sooner did he open the back door and Finney was right there to greet him. He reached down and pet the dog. "Okay, now go lay down." The dog whined and walked away.

What Lee didn't take into consideration before entering the home was an unexpected visitor. He proceeded up the stairs to Daisy's bedroom. These cottages all had similar layouts, which he was familiar with. He assumed her bedroom was in the loft.

Lee opened the drawers one by one, and ran his fingers through the clothes, feeling for a stone. He glanced under the bed and saw nothing. Next, he walked over to the tall wardrobe and ran his hands through the dresses that hung on a bar. He inspected the shelf. "No sign of a stone anywhere. How unusual. Where did she put it?"

Grace passed by Daisy's house every morning on her way to school. She hoped her friend would be waiting on her front lawn like old times. To her disappointment, there was no sign of Daisy three days in a row.

"It's a new week," she told Thomas as they strolled down Daisy's block. If she's not waiting for us, I'm going to the door to plead with her to come to school, and I'm not taking no for an answer.

Lee, still snooping in Daisy's room, heard the screen door screech and several loud knocks. He stayed put and listened.

Grace opened the door, and Finney, who was lying on the floor by the sofa, rushed to the door and sprang up on her hind legs to greet her.

Lee took a quick look at the door. "Dang!" He whispered and moved silently down the steps while keeping his eye on the dog and the girl. Luckily for him, Finney was blocking Grace's view and Lee was able to sneak out the back door without being seen. Or so he thought.

The moment Grace looked up to wipe Finney's saliva off her face, she caught a glimpse of someone running out the back door. Finney turned away and barked in the same direction. "Whoever that was shouldn't have been here. I'm sure of it," she thought.

Grace panicked and slammed the door shut. She

grabbed Thomas' hand. "Hurry, Thomas! We must go." They both escaped across the front lawn before turning onto the sidewalk. Grace was walking too fast for Thomas, but she continued to pull him along with her.

"Grace, I'm scared," he cried out. "Everything will be okay if we hurry. I need to find Daisy stat. "I sure hope she's in school today." Grace muttered.

Even though the school was on the small side, the girls were not in the same class. Grace crossed her fingers that she'd be able to find Daisy before the bell rang.

She dropped Thomas off by the boys' entrance before heading over to the picnic area in search of her friend. "Oh! There she is." Grace quickened her step until she reached the oak tree where a group of girls sat talking.

"Daisy! You're here." The friends exchanged hugs. "I need to borrow her for a second." Grace told the other girls as she grabbed Daisy's hand.

"I went to your house this morning and saw someone sneaking out your back door." She spoke in a panic. Daisy moved her hand in a brushing off gesture.

"Probably my father," she spoke calmly.

"No. I'm positive it was not Mr. Wilhelm," replied Grace, still jumpy.

Daisy furrowed her brow and considered this information. Her stomach got a little queasy as she wondered if her kidnapper finally located her. *Might it be him? After all these years?* "Should we call my mother and tell her? I'm sure we can use the telephone in the office."

The girls raced into the office and explained they had an urgent need to call home, and asked to use the telephone. The school secretary looked at them with a peculiar eye and pointed to the wall. "Make it quick," she advised.

"I'm unaware of our phone number." Daisy felt

embarrassed. "That's okay. Ask the operator to connect you." Daisy looked curiously at the old-fashioned phone, put the receiver near her ear, then leaned close to the mouthpiece that resembled a small megaphone. She whispered into the opening.

"Here, give the phone to me," said Grace, rather impatiently. "Hello operator, please connect me to Katherine Wilhelm." She glanced at Daisy. "It's ringing." When Katherine answered, Grace explained the entire scenario of the morning in detail. She hung up the phone and repeated the conversation to Daisy.

"Your mom thinks it could have been your father. He often forgets things and has to go back home. She'll double check with him later." "This person was shorter than your father. And why would Mr. Wilhelm rush out the door and not say hello? I'm certain he saw me standing there." Daisy took in a deep breath. "Let's not panic yet."

She pulled Grace's arm and led her back to the bench by the oak tree. "We still have a few minutes left before the bell rings. Let's join the others."

After school, the usual three; Grace, Daisy, and Thomas walked home like old times. Today, instead of Daisy going to Grace's house, Daisy insisted her friend come to hers. Thomas continued home when the girls disappeared into the house. As always, with the sound of the screen door screeching open, Finney greeted them.

Katherine came out of the kitchen to say hello, her apron covered in flour hand prints. "Would you like some lemonade? Sure is hot out today, huh?" The girls looked at each other and replied in unison, "nah".

"Mother. Did you find out if father left through the back door this morning?" "I'm waiting for him to arrive home and then I will ask him." Daisy continued to worry that one day her kidnapper would locate her. She tried to settle her beating heart by whispering, "It's okay, it's not him." "Daisy, are you alright?" Asked Katherine. "Your face looks pale." "Yes. I'm fine." She smiled, grabbed Grace's hand, and the two girls hurried up the stairs, and Katherine resumed her baking.

Normally, Daisy kept her room spotless. She hated clutter and believed everything had its place. A good habit she picked up from Grace years ago. Today, though, the room was completely turned upside down. "Daisy, was there a knockout, drag down fight in here?" "No!" She replied. "I didn't do any of this. I never leave my drawers or my wardrobe open, and things scattered about.— Mommmm!"

Katherine rushed up the stairs and appeared quite disturbed at the sight of Daisy's room. "What happened in here?" Her jaw dropped. "That's what we were wondering." Grace stood with her arms crossed. "I told you someone was in here this morning. Nobody believed me."

"Why would someone need to rummage around in Daisy's room? What could they possibly be looking for in here?" Katherine was shocked. "Did you check to see if anything's missing?" Katherine asked with concern.

"No, I haven't searched yet." Daisy went straight to the open wardrobe and glanced around. She moved her dresses aside, then nonchalantly peered down at the bottom where she kept her camera, and hoped her diary was still hidden in the case. She closed the door.

The dresser draws were left open by whoever was in

the room, and pieces of clothing strewn about. No sign of the Levi jeans. Suddenly, Daisy felt a sharp twist in her gut, brought on by anxiety no doubt. "I feel ill." Daisy covered her mouth and ran downstairs to the bathroom.

Several minutes later she reappeared at the bottom of the steps. "It was a mild case of dry heaves and nothing more." Daisy shouted.

Katherine was already making her way down the stairs. "I'll pour you a glass of ginger ale. That'll help your stomach." "Thank you, mom."

"Daisy, I'll stay and help you tidy up in here." Grace was already folding clothes and placing them neatly back into the drawers when she came across a pair of what looked like boys pants. "What are these?" She asked herself.

"What are what?" Daisy asked as she entered the room. Grace held up the Levi jeans. Daisy let out a big sigh of relief and quickly swiped the pants from Grace. "I'll tell you all about these, later." She looked to make sure Katherine wasn't standing there. "Mom!" Daisy yelled down the stairs. "Grace is going to help me clean up."

"Okay, we'll talk to your father when he gets home. He may want us to report this. I'm going to take Finney for a short walk now."

ʇWENTY ONE

SECRETS REVEALED

Daisy retrieved her camera case from the wardrobe floor and motioned for Grace to sit on the bed, then plopped down next to her. "Okay, I have lots to reveal, but only if you promise not to tell anyone.

And, you must give me your word that you'll be objective and keep an open mind."

"Is this about your disappearance?" Grace asked. "Yes. And you're the only one in the entire world I trust to share this with. Let's pinky promise." And they did.

Daisy led with an explanation. "This is going to sound genuinely crazy, but is 100% the truth." "You've won my interest. I'm listening."

"I learned something fascinating about the sacred site. It IS an old burial ground. BUT — there's more to it." She touched the blond streak in Grace's hair, and twirled it around her finger, recalling the woman she met at Carver's. "WHAT? Tell me." "I'm getting to that, but it's really a bizarre story."

Daisy rested the camera case on her lap. She opened it, peeked up at Grace, and asked, "do you ever consider what the future will be like?" Grace thought about the question. "Sometimes I wonder, yes. I imagine myself marrying the cutest boy in school and raising my children in the same house I live in now." Daisy rolled her eyes and pulled out the color postcard of Carver's luncheonette from the case.

"Close your eyes and try to imagine yourself 25 years in the future." Daisy spoke in a quiet mysterious voice. Grace giggled. "What color car do you drive? What do you do for fun?" "This is silly. What does this have to do with your disappearance?" Asked Grace. "Brace yourself, I have something to show you."

Daisy handed the postcard to Grace. "Does anything in this photo seem odd or familiar?" Grace took the postcard and studied the image. "I see a luncheonette. Nothing unusual about that," she replied. Daisy shook her head and pointed at the card. "Look right here, the side of this building. It's the paper mill. Don't you recognize it?" Grace squinted her eyes while she examined the photo. "And look at this automobile." Daisy tapped her finger at the bright red Chevy Bel Air in the foreground of the parking lot.

"Where did you get this card?" Asked Grace. Daisy rolled her hand. "Turn it over." Grace read the address on the back of the card. "125 Crosswood Drive. But there isn't a luncheonette on Crosswood." "There will be in the future. Right next to the paper mill."

"Daisy, you sound ridiculous. Tell me where you got the card."

Daisy stood up and focused on the little window, wishing it was lower so she could see out to the street. "I bought it at the luncheonette for five cents." Grace fell back on the bed and let out the biggest laugh.

Daisy pulled the Levi jeans out of the drawer. "These are mine. I was wearing them the day Officer Cuish found me. She slipped off her skirt and put the pants on. "There! Have you ever seen me wear these before? Or have you ever seen a girl wear these before?" Grace had the most perturbed look on her face. "Daisy, take those off. You look ridiculous. What's that got to do with the postcard?"

Daisy plopped down on the bed, rested her elbows on her thighs and held her head in her hands. She felt defeated. The one person she thought she could trust with her biggest truth, her best friend in the world, was humiliating her. "Daiz, what's wrong?" Just then, Katherine called from downstairs. "Grace, honey, your mom wants you home now."

"Don't go yet." Daisy sat down on the bed and put her hand on Grace's leg. "I have more I want to show you." She picked through the case, deciding if she should show Grace the photo of Walter and her, or the money. She pulled a few dollar bills out of the case. "Look at the date," she said, pointing to the bottom of the bill. "Series 1950." Grace read out loud. "Daisy, where did you get this money, and the postcard?"

Katherine appeared at the bottom of the stairs and called again for Grace. "Daisy, I've gotta go now. I'll see you tomorrow? And then you can tell me exactly what kind of prank you're pulling."

Daisy felt the frustration deep inside her chest. She was so excited about telling her best friend in the world every single detail of her travel experience, and now she was forced to wait.

She stood up and paced the room. "Don't wear those silly pants, okay?" Ordered Grace. "Seriously? You're making fun of me now? If you're going to make jokes, maybe I won't confide in you anymore."

April 2, 1925

Dear Diary -

I'm back from another bizarre adventure. I don't know how I got so lucky, but I was able to return to 1925. Some months are unaccounted for, but that's okay. I'm with my family again and that's all I wanted. Oh - and - guess what? We finally have a telephone in the house! And —there are new photos hanging on the wall. One is of Katherine cradling a young girl, who looks so familiar. But I'm not sure where I saw her before.

PS. Something strange occurred today. Someone snuck into the house and messed around in my room. I don't believe anything, was taken though. I fear it could be the same man who kidnapped me.
It's possible he's a time traveler, too. And perhaps that's why he camped near that mysterious wall.
I'm prepared to watch my back from now on! Supper is ready. I have to go. Will write more later.

Daisy

TWENTY TWO

ARE YOU A TIME TRAVELER?

Daisy woke up with an amusing thought after being told by Grace that her Levi jeans looked silly. School couldn't come quick enough as far as she was concerned. "Let's see what everyone thinks about a girl wearing long pants to school." She spoke softly in a snarky tone as she slipped into her golden era jeans.

Daisy raced down the stairs and out the door as soon as she heard Katherine leave the house. She left later than usual, but made up for it by walking fast.

Daisy could hear the first bell ring as she came around the corner. She climbed the stairs two at a time, arriving at the front door just as the second bell began to ring. "Daisy Wilhelm! You're late." Reprimanded the head master... aka Principal Persnickety. (A nickname given to him by students in the past.)

"Yes sir. May I have permission to go?" "Tardiness is not to be taken lightly around here, so no, you may not be excused. But more importantly, what are you wearing on your legs?" "These are long pants, sir. Levi Jeans." "Yes, I noticed. But WHY are you wearing them? Girls may not wear pants to school. You should know the dress code." "Yes, sir. I made a mistake." "You certainly did. Now go home and change. And, make sure this never happens again or I'll be phoning your mother."

Daisy walked away from the head-master in a true teenage huff. Her arms swinging in the air as she groaned. "Stupid dress codes! Such hullabaloo." Her walk home wasn't more than a half mile, but still she chose a short-cut through Mrs. Greene's back yard. Climbing over a three foot high fence wearing long pants was a breeze. "I'd never be able to cut through yards and jump fences in a skirt." Daisy snapped in protest.

Lee Gives It One More Try

Parked far enough down the street to be out of view, Lee surveyed the cottage from his car. "I've got one more shot to find that stone without being seen." Under his watchful eye, he witnessed the family leave the house and five minutes later made his move. Lee walked up to the front door and pretended to knock, in case any of the neighbors were watching. He turned the knob and stepped inside.

Finney was lying on a beam of sunlight in the kitchen. She was sound asleep and never heard the door or the steps creak as Lee made his way up to the loft.

The Unexpected Break-In

Daisy entered the home and hurried up the stairs so fast it wasn't possible for Lee to hide, so both were startled when they came face to face.

"What are you doing here?" Her heart raced as she stood by the doorway.

"I'm sorry for the intrusion, Daisy. I'm embarrassed you caught me but I have a good explanation." Lee put his hands in his pockets and got a little too close for her comfort.

"Oh yea? Well, start explaining!" Daisy gave him her most intense glare, crossed her arms, and waited.

"I believe you have something that I need to take a closer look at." *Whoa! Did Grace tell him about the postcard or the money?* She picked at her bottom lip.

"Please sit. This is important." He explained. "I don't wanna sit. You need to leave." "I won't leave until I get what I came here for." She wondered if he noticed her shaking.

"What do you need to see so desperately that you broke into my house? Why didn't you ask about this yesterday when you were here? Huh?" Lee replied. "It was my intention to be discreet. I didn't want to get your parents involved."

Daisy twirled her hair around her forefinger while she thought about the secrets she shared with Grace. "I have nothing here that concerns you, so get out of my house." Daisy pointed to the door.

"Listen, Daisy. The day I picked you up and brought you home, I saw you place a stone on the table."

The stone? That's what he wants? Not the postcard or the money? Either way, I'm screwed. She challenged him. "I don't know what stone you're talking about." "Yes, you do. Why don't you stop being so stubborn and hand it over so I can leave?" "What's makes it so special that you want it so badly?"

Lee took a deep breath and composed himself. "It has a distinctive symbol engraved into it, and I want to examine it more closely to confirm my suspicions." "Suspicions about what?" She asked. He was agitated and tired of her little game. "Oh. I have a hunch you're aware of its power." Daisy raised her right brow. *Holy moly. He knows.*

Lee faced the wall and tilted his head toward the sunlight coming through the window. "I'm gonna tell you a story." He turned and faced Daisy. She sat down on the bed. Tilted her head to the right and clasped her hands together. *This had better be good.* "Okay, I'm listening."

Hearing voices, Finney kerplunk'd up the stairs and barked to show her excitement. She loved people. Lee waited for the dog to settle down before he began.

"The Sunday before Easter, when I was eight years old, my parents, aunts, and uncles, cousins, and myself went to Live Oak Park for a family picnic. Something we did often and always the same routine; The women spread out a big tablecloth and placed the food on it. Cold boiled chicken, potato salad, bread and scones. Everyone sat around the blanket and talked and ate. It was a tradition to go for a canoe ride on the river after we finished eating.

"On this particular day, something terrible happened. Our dog took off chasing a squirrel, so my father ran after him. When they failed to return, the older cousins began a search." Daisy listened. "I remember that day, but too young to recall the details. I'm retelling the story as it was told to me years later.

They found the dog sniffing around the sacred burial site by the big wall, but my father was never located. They assumed he was attacked by a bear and dragged away." "Why would they think that?" Asked Daisy. "Because at the time, before expansive land development at the river, bears, foxes, deer and many other animals lived in the forest. Not so much now, but 25 years ago it was." *Oh boy.* She thought. "Just wait until they see how the development progresses in 50 years."

"Well, regardless, what does this have to do with a rock you think I have?" Her foot fidgeted back and forth, shaking the bed.

"Daisy, I know you have the travel stone. I saw it with my own eyes." Daisy yawned. "I think my father may be a time traveler, and he could be stuck in another decade, unable to return."

He sat next to Daisy on the bed and faced her. "I've done plenty of research which backs up what I'm speculating happened. There's an unexplainable force from the wall which gets activated when someone picks up the travel stone." "Anyone?" Asked Daisy. "No. I think only certain people who have this inherited trait. And I'd prefer to think my father is one of those people, rather than think, he got eaten by a bear. I must find out if I can travel too, so I can locate him." Daisy pitied him.

"Can I ask you a question in confidence?" Lee asked. Daisy shook her head yes. "Okay, what?" "Are you a time traveler?" When she didn't respond, he continued. "You disappeared for almost a year with no explanation as to where you were. Why is that?" Her attention was drawn to images in her head from the day of her abduction in 1972.

"How do I know you're not going to bring me straight to some looney bin if I tell you anything?" He laughed heartily. "What looney bin? You definitely don't belong in a looney bin, if there is such a place." His laugh continued for several minutes.

Daisy had no intention of revealing anything about her travels, but wanted this back-and-forth scenario to cease. She stood up and walked over to her wardrobe, reached down to the bottom, and pulled out the stone. "Here you go." Daisy held the stone in her palm and waited for Lee to take it. "If you mention this to anyone, I will deny everything you say." "Fair enough," he replied, and made a zipped lip gesture with his fingers.

"Does this stone always feel hot?" He asked. "Yes. Put it down until you're ready to go." He shoved the treasure into his police jacket. "I hope you find your father Officer Cuish." "Thank you. Me too."

April 3, 1925

Dear Diary -

Just when I thought things couldn't get any weirder around here, I come home to find Officer Cuish snooping around in my loft. LOOKING FOR MY TRAVEL STONE! Is this another NON-Coincidence happening?
I remember the day Walter and I realized something plopped us into each other's lives for a reason, and he explained there are no coincidences. It's FATE!
Did fate bring Lee Cuish into my life?
Whatever for?

Daisy

TWENTY THREE

NO PRANKS

Dreamy Al Gibson from the candy store, knocked on the Wilhelms' front door. "Al? What are YOU doing here?"

As long as she'd known him he never came to her house. Why would he? They barely knew each other. "Well, I heard you were back, and I wanted to ask if I can walk you to school today?" *He's such a hunk.* A dark shade of pink filled her cheeks. "Oh. Okay. That would be nice. I'll grab my things and be right out."

A center on the school basketball team, and considered one of the popular students, Al towered over her, and most of the girls. He was tall, athletic, and handsome.

She delighted in her new acquaintance and the attention from him, but also knew she wouldn't dare let him get too close to her heart. *I'm almost certain this is the man Grace marries in the future.* She thought back to the day at Carver's Luncheonette. *How can I know for sure?* She bit her lip and stared ahead.

Random puddles and morning mist were all that remained from the previous night's storm. The two walked slowly down Riverside Drive breathing in the fresh smelling grass and being careful not to get their feet wet.

Daisy mentioned nothing about her disappearance

and he never asked. He expressed he missed seeing her around school and in the candy store. "I'm glad you're back Daisy." He gave her a side eye glance. Daisy giggled.

"Al, does your whole family work at the store?" Her reasons for prying were valid. "It's just my parents who manage the store. I help out when I can." *This information confirms my suspicion; he has no brothers. But what about other male Gibsons in town about the same age as us? How can I possibly figure out if this is the Gibson Grace marries?*

"How's your friend Grace?" He asked. "She's well." Daisy narrowed her eyes. "Does she have a boyfriend?" Daisy raised her right brow. *So all this flirting with me was to get the particulars on Grace? At least he could have waited until we were further along in our walk. Geeze! That's bold!* She struggled to keep her cool. "No, I don't believe she does. You interested?" Her cheeky question caught him off guard and he didn't answer.

When they arrived at school, Al pointed to the boys entrance. "That's me." He titled his head down far enough to connect with Daisy's eyes. "It has been a pleasure to walk with you this morning. Thank you, Daisy." "Why does he have to be so damn charming?"

After school, Grace found Daisy and they walked home together. "Al Gibson offered to walk me home today." She paused to hear Daisy's thoughts. "He wants to ask you out." Replied Daisy. "Me? I thought his interest was in you?" "Nope. Apparently, he's too much of a coward to talk to you." Both girls laughed. "Well, he is easy on the eyes. But if you like him, Daisy, I'll tell him I'm spoken for." Said Grace. "No. Are you kidding? I've got no time for boys right now."

The two walked in silence for the next block. When they approached Daisy's house, Grace asked, "Daisy, are you inviting me in? Not to talk about Al, but to get the details about your disappearance." Her face lit up with excitement. "So much to tell you." She pulled on her friend's hand and led her through the front door.

The girls galloped up the stairs with excitement. Grace kicked off her shoes before dropping backwards onto the bed. "Move over," pleaded Daisy as she waved with her free hand. In the other, her camera case and the Levi Jeans she wore the previous day.

Grace turned on her side and dangled her feet off the edge of the bed. "Okay, where were we?" Asked Daisy. "Oh yes, mocking these denim pants. Here, look at the tag. Girls size 12." Grace sat up and examined the pants. "I didn't doubt the pants were for girls. I'm sure somewhere on a farm in Iowa a girl is wearing a pair just like these." "Oh, don't be so close minded. This is a popular style of clothing in the 1940s and 50s. And beyond." Grace laughed.

"Here, try them on." "Okay." Grace hopped off the bed and slipped the jeans on under her skirt. Then she admired her butt in the mirror. "Oh, these are nice. Very flattering. You've piqued my interest Daisy, so please, go on. Tell me more about your time travel experience."

Daisy rolled her eyes at Grace's sarcastic tone. She sat down next to her friend and pulled out the postcard again. They went over all the details of the front, then flipped the card over to peep the back. "C.D. Wilhelm Photo Studio. 1945." Daisy pointed to the line of text.

"Oh my stars." Grace stroked her chin. "This is unimaginable." "I know! It's been freaking me out, Grace." "And, you're definitely not pulling a prank on me?" "NO! Stop with the prank pulling. I'm telling you, as far-fetched as this sounds, this is all true."

Daisy pulled out the photo of her and Walter. "I ended up in an orphanage when no one came forward to claim me. This is where I met Walter. The nephew of Gertie. "What? My Gertie? Our cook?" Grace exclaimed as she pulled the photo from Daisy's hand and held it to her eyes. "Yes. Same woman.

Anyway, Walter disappeared the same way I did. At the wall by the sacred site. He's been at the orphanage since 1940. Well, 1915 in our time."

"What are the possibilities?" Grace reacted with question. "That's what I'm trying to figure out. And that's not all." Grace paid close attention. "Did you see the photo of a little girl downstairs on the wall?" "Yes. Who is she?" "I haven't a clue. Katherine said her name is Marion, but never told me anything more. And, I'm sure she lived at the same orphanage long before I arrived." "Really? How would you know?"

"In the entrance hall at the orphanage I saw a bulletin board with the photos of five children, including me, who were never claimed by family. With the name of each child and year they arrived at the orphanage written at the bottom of the photo. Three year old Mari arrived in 1930. Walter is on the board as well. I have a photo! - And, that reminds me. I must develop a copy and get it to Gertie."

"Could the little girl be Katherine and Charles' daughter?" "I would assume so. If not, she must've been someone special, like a close relative. The names are similar."

Daisy filled Grace in on what she had already concluded. "And Katherine was so adamant about us not going near that sacred site." "Maybe she thought we would disappear too?" Asked Grace. Daisy shrugged her shoulders.

"There are no photos of Marion older than age three. It could be possible that she disappeared around 1920 and time traveled ahead 10 years to 1930. That's assuming I've got the dates correct." Grace nodded in agreement.

If Marion, is Mari, and she disappeared at three years old, it very well could be the same girl."

Grace added to the theory. "In the photos downstairs, Katherine appears to be about the same age as she is right now, so they probably weren't taken too long ago."

"And when I arrived in 1922, Charles told me they had no children." Daisy added.

The girls were moving around the small room to get the blood flowing to their brains. A common exercise to help one think. So they thought.

"Can I see the photo you referenced? The one that shows Marion on the missing children's board?" "Yes!" Daisy pulled it out of her camera case and handed it to Grace.

"Can you enlarge this? It's hard to see details." "Exactly what I was thinking! I'll do that Saturday when Katherine and Charles go to the community dance, and I can sneak into his darkroom."

Grace pulled the jeans-from-the-future off and folded them.

"Does everyone really wear these in the future?" "Yes! And, other cool styles too. You'll see."

"I'm still trying to wrap my head around the idea that you actually did travel through time.

...It's just surreal.

Do you possess some special type of power?" Grace didn't know what to think at this point.

"I don't know for sure how I did it.

In my research I learned that some Native American people from this area possessed special traits. One of them being able to travel through time, using a special stone or a wall as a time portal."

"Like the wall you found on your hike?" "Yes. That one.

And, I honestly can't say whether I acquired that trait from my father because I'm not sure of his ethnicity. It may be something else entirely. I do know that I want to figure it out someday."

"So, what do you do now? About Marion?"

"I wait until 1930 and go to the orphanage to find out more about her."

"You're going to wait five long years?"

"Yes. What other choice do I have?

Should I tell my parents I'm a time traveler and I know where their daughter is, but they can't be reunited until 1930?"

"No! Ha! That won't be received well.

But in the meantime, for our own peace of mind, lets check the birth announcements from old newspapers at the library." Exclaimed Grace. "We'll be able to find out if Katherine and Charles announced the birth of a child!"

"OR!" Daisy had a thought. "Maybe I shouldn't wait until 1930." "What do you mean by that? Don't do anything stupid Daisy."

"You're right. Picking up another rock. Dumb idea."

Twenty Four

ONE MYSTERY SOLVED

April 21, 1925

Dear Diary,

I was able to enlarge the photo of Mari, and we definitely see a resemblance between her and Marion. It breaks my heart that I can't tell Katherine and Charles what I know. Grace and I both agree the best way to handle this is to wait until 1930.

I also developed a duplicate of the photo I took of Walter for Gertie. Grace is going to slip the photo and the letter from Walter into Gertie's incoming mail pile when she isn't home. I'm relieved that the mystery of his disappearance was solved and Gertie can find hope that she'll see him again in the future.

Daisy

As the ninth grade banquet approached it marked the end of an era for their studies.

Grace would continue her education through high school, taking the courses required for admission to a university. Her future plans included earning a degree in home economics and then marriage and children.

Daisy, on the other hand, had no desire to attend university. Her heart was set on learning the trade of photography and working as an apprentice for Charles.

"Daisy I need you to hold still. I'm almost finished pinning this sleeve." "Mother, Grace will be here any minute." "Do you want a new dress for your 9th grade banquet, or not?" Daisy smiled sincerely. "Of course."

Grace knocked loudly on the Wilhelm's front door and then barged right in. "DAISY! I'm here. Are you ready to go to the library?" Daisy stepped off the stool she'd been standing on for the last twenty minutes while Katherine was making the final alterations on her dress. "Mom, can I go?"

ANOTHER MYSTERY SOLVED

At the library, Daisy turned to Grace. "Now we have our answer." Their search ended in a newspaper dated January 21, 1917. "This confirms my suspicion about Mari. And now – I know what I have to do."

Births
Wilhelm – Charles and Elizabeth,
193 Riverside Drive. Girl.

EPIGRAPH

Charles and Daisy grinned from ear to ear while they admired the newly hung sign next to their front door.

C.D. WILHELM PHOTOGRAPHY
EST. 1930

"The perfect addition to our new home, don't you think?" "Yes." Replied Daisy, and added, "you manifested a bigger house and your own photo business before you turned 40. And you did it!"

Charles laid the hammer on the ground and reached his arm towards Daisy to shake hands.

"Partners?" Daisy confirmed. "Partners indeed!"

"And how special that our first client is your best friend's wedding." "She knows I'm the best." Daisy punched her dad's arm lightly and laughed at her arrogant remark. "Thanks for all the training years, dad. I was lucky to be your apprentice. And I sincerely wish that one day I am as skilled as you." Charles side hugged his daughter after he wiped a tear from his eye.

"I'm ecstatic for Grace and Al. They make such a lovely couple and I have a hunch they will have a wonderful future." "Oh, you have a hunch do you? Sometimes I wonder about your keen intuition." Daisy chuckled quietly.

"I've gotta run. Mom is finishing my dress today and then I have some errands to run before the big day tomorrow." Monday would also be a big day, but that was Daisy's secret for now.

In a ceremony Sunday, July 6th, in First Presbyterian Church, Miss Grace Dalton was married to Albert Gibson by the Rev. Joe Kelly.

The bride is the daughter of Huxley and Elizabeth Dalton of Reef Rd. The bridegroom's parents are Mr. and Mrs. Paul Gibson of Mortimer Ave.

Miss Daisy Wilhelm was the bride's attendant, and the brides brother Thomas Dalton was best man.

The bride wore an elegant champagne silk dress with an empire waist, featuring gorgeous beadwork from front to back. Her bouquet was a shower of red and pink roses. Miss Wilhelm wore a tea length pinkish beige chiffon dress with polka dot accents. She carried an arm bouquet of pink roses.

The bride is a graduate of Finch College in Manhattan. The groom is currently a student at Montclair State University where he plays point guard for the men's basketball team.

The couple will reside on Reef Rd. in Rutherford.

JULY 7, 1930

Daisy checked the bus schedule one more time. She'd been waiting five years for this day and was anxious.

If Mari hasn't arrived at the orphanage yet I may have to come up with another plan. I'll cross that bridge when I get to it.

After a twenty minute ride to Passaic, Daisy exited the bus and continued walking several blocks until she reached St. Mary's Orphanage.

Standing in front of her previous temporary dwelling place made the hairs on her arms stand up. *This is surreal. Did I really and truly live here in the future?*

My plan is to inquire about any children under the age of five who may be here. I'll pretend I'm writing an article on missing children. I doubt Sister Lorraine or Sister Maria will be suspicious. Both sweet ladies who trusted everyone.

If Mari isn't here I'll check the photo board. There's a good chance she arrived later in the year. And in that case, I may have to come up with plan B.

A middle aged woman dressed in a nun's habit opened the door. "Hello dear. What can I do for you?" "Hi Sister. My name is Daisy. I'm a student, and here to inquire about missing children for an article I'm writing." "Oh, is that right? I'm very pleased to make your acquaintance Daisy. I'm Sister Lorraine. Please come in."

Daisy looked around the familiar corridor while they walked to Sister Lorraine's office. Memories of an older nun and what seemed to be another lifetime flooded her mind.

Just as they entered the office Daisy saw the photo board hanging on the far wall behind the Sister's desk. She squinted her eyes for better focus but the lone photo was too small to see from where she was standing.

"Please sit." Daisy wanted to push past her and go directly to the photo board but she didn't want to come across as rude. "Thank you. I think I will."

"Now then. What paper did you say you write for?" "I didn't actually. It's for my college entrance exam. I have a passion for helping destitute children. Writing about orphans is one of the topics I'm including in my paper." *I hope she buys this story.*

"Well, if you're looking for orphans you've come to the right place. What exactly would you like to know for your article?"

"Specifically, I'm interested in writing about children who have no known next of kin, and how they came to live here."

"I commend your enthusiasm for writing on this topic but I'm afraid there won't be much to say. All, but one of the children here do have family. Some are here temporarily while their parents get back on their feet, and others have family who are just too poor to take care of them." "It's hard to imagine such sadness, Sister."

Daisy thought this would be an easy morning, but instead it brought on dreadful feelings of the unknown. *What if I hadn't been adopted by the Wilhelms? Would I be one of the orphans living my life out here at St. Marys?* She held a blank stare until Sister Lorraine stood up and interrupted her trance.

"Come with me. I'll introduce you to a young girl who was found wandering around in a park near Waterloo. She's been with us two weeks, and so far, no one has come to claim her."

⁓℮⁓

"Daisy. I'd like you to meet Mari." Daisy's heart skipped a beat. She bent down to the little girl's eye level and smiled.

Daisy has a successful photography business, and the loving family she always wished for. But there are still some unanswered queries from her past.

Will she embrace
the life she has now,
or risk losing it all
on a daring decision?

Follow Daisy into adulthood and perhaps a different century, when the story continues in book two.

Ivy Lighton